# CLOCK

## CARON BUTLER
## AND JUSTIN A. REYNOLDS

KATHERINE TEGEN BOOKS

*An Imprint of HarperCollins Publishers*

Library of Congress Cataloging-in-Publication Data

Names: Butler, Caron, 1980– author. | Reynolds, Justin A., author.
Title: Shot clock / Caron Butler and Justin A. Reynolds.
Description: First edition. | New York, NY : Katherine Tegen Books, [2022] |
    Audience: Ages 8-12. | Audience: Grades 4-6. | Summary: After the death
    of his friend, Tony must work to make the basketball team, but when he gets
    the chance to join the squad as statistician, he must grapple with honoring the
    memory of his basketball-loving friend while also trying to fit in on the team.
Identifiers: LCCN 2022000157 | ISBN 978-0-06-306959-6 (hardcover)
Subjects: CYAC: Basketball—Fiction. | Grief—Fiction. | Police
    shootings—Fiction. | LCGFT: Sports fiction. | Novels.
Classification: LCC PZ7.1.B8927 Sh 2022 | DDC [Fic]—dc23
LC record available at https://lccn.loc.gov/2022000157

Typography by Joel Tippie
22 23 24 25 26   PC/LSCH   10 9 8 7 6 5 4 3 2 1
❖
First Edition

*To every kid wondering if you can change the game . . .*
*YOU CAN.*

SHOT
CLOCK

# THE WARM-UP

It's two against one.

Not that it matters.

The twins were trash-talking all day at school, saying Dante should just punk out now, save himself the humiliation.

"The hurting we gon' put on you, man, like, I *almost* feel bad," the slightly taller twin says as he checks the ball to start the game.

"It's not gon' be like last time, bruh," the other twin promises. "We really 'bout to mop you, D."

But D doesn't snap back. Just smiles like he knows something they don't.

But I know, too.

D was the number-two-ranked high school player in the whole country last year. As a sophomore. But this past year, I watched him elevate his game to new heights, Sunday through Saturday, he *put in work*—days drenched in sweat during the July heat wave, December nights half-frozen as we shoveled mountains of wet snow off Paradise Court so he could work on his footwork.

I was right there with him. Putting up thousands—no, *tens of thousands*—of shots, zigzagging around the orange cones Coach James gave D, dragging the dirty orange construction barrels from the potholes they weren't fixing on Ellison Ave and pretending they were defenders, hurdling them as we knifed in for layups, corkscrewed for one-handed floaters.

Some nights it'd be raining so hard Mom made me stay in—said, *What kind of ball player you gonna be when you catch pneumonia, Tone?*—and I wondered if D was gonna skip practice, too, but then, from my bed, my window slightly open, I'd hear:

*Chu-kaa.*

*Chu-kaa.*

*Chu-kaa.*

Most nights I listened to D dance all over the court till my eyes were too heavy to keep open. The sounds, always the same.

*Thwack, thwack, shwerrrp, chu-kaa.*

Translation: dribble, dribble, spin + pull-up, swish.

4

Or *thwack, thwack, crrnch-crrnch, chu-kaa.*

Translation: dribble, dribble, stepback, swish.

The crunch only happening when you were on the north end of the court, where the concrete's crumbled so bad it's basically gravel. But whatever, that's not stopping anybody from jab-stepping behind the spray-painted three-point line and splashing on whoever wants it—

Especially when the ball's in D's hands.

Like now.

I told Mom I pushed my bed under the window so I could catch the breeze because in the summertime it's hot enough to melt an ice cream truck, but to be real, I just wanted to be able to sit in bed and watch the court. Sometimes I pretend my fourth-story bedroom is the Fiserv Forum—where the Milwaukee Bucks play—and I'm sitting way up in one of those skyboxes like a celebrity. I act like the TV cameras are aimed at me, and I smile and salute, or I make as if I'm so into the game I don't even notice them.

But the twins? They are most definitely noticing D right now.

No question he has their *undivided* attention.

Every time the ball leaves D's hands, people standing around the court chime *cha-ching, cha-ching,* like the cash register at the corner store; that's how money D's jumper is. Sometimes he doesn't even watch it sail through the net . . . he's already walking back to the line for his next possession, updating the score:

*6–1, me.*

*7–1, me.*

*8–2, me.*

But sometimes D pauses to admire his work, his eyes following the ball's perfect arc, its beautiful rotation, until it splashes through the tattered nylon.

Every time his new KDs leave the asphalt, it's like he's launching into space, his chest square, elbows bent, ball rolling off his long fingertips.

You match up against D, the outcome is always the same. Like watching reruns of your favorite show. It's just a matter of *how you want it.*

That's about as much trash talk as D serves up.

That and his other favorite phrase: *all day.*

As in, *I can do this all day.*

D will put you on skates with his crossover, then pull back and wait for you to regain your balance—and you know he could've blown past you and gotten to the rack, but he's toying with you. And after you pick yourself off the ground, dust the gravel from your knees, he looks you dead in your scared eyes, and asks, *How you want it?*

As in, *You want this jumper?*

*You want this dribble drive?*

*You want this spin move, up and under?*

I'm telling you—I've seen this episode so many times.


**THE INTRODUCTION:** Some dude swears on his mama he's gonna lock D up, all *He ain't about to get nan points on me,* *watch*—and then D working the perimeter, launching jumper after jumper dead in the defender's grill. *Cha-ching, chu-kaa.*

**THE CONFLICT:** Now the defender's all in his feelings cuz everybody's posting his butt-whupping on the Gram, plus they're oohing and aahing and cackling, and D's not even saying nothing cuz his game is his mouth, but the defender's heated, like, *Whatever, man, all he got is that pull-up, bring that weak stuff in the paint, see if I don't swat it five hundred light-years into the future.*

**THE RESOLUTION:** D only smiles, then goes right at dude with an array of spin moves so dazzling he's got washers and dryers drooling—finishing with every kind of layup, left hand, right hand, up and under, off glass, every angle. *All day*, D says softly, walking back to check-ball. *So, how you want it now?*

But sometimes, every now and then, the defender timed his jump perfectly with D's, the defender's long arm stretching, his fingers reaching to reject D's layup. He's happy—you can see it on his face—because he's finally about to shut D up, *put THIS on YouTube*, he's thinking . . . only to see his eyes widen in surprise the moment he realizes that while he's on his way back to the concrete without even getting a fingernail on the ball, D's still rising, elevating, the kid practically levitating, up up up, the sun over his shoulder gleaming bright enough to make everybody squint, the ball scooped between D's wrist and forearm, the two halves of his body seemingly going in opposite directions, before he lets the ball glide off his fingers, spiraling as it kisses high off the backboard. The net doesn't even move as the ball slips through.

That's the thing about D.

He has *everything* going for him.

Handles, deadly jumper, range for days, the kind of suffocating defense that made the dudes he was guarding mad frustrated.

D's built for this game.

Tall, strong, crazy quick.

He jumps out the gym.

Seriously, nobody gets up like D.

Nobody.

So, who would've guessed that only a few hours later, D wouldn't get up at all?

# 1ST QUARTER

Sleeping's my superpower.

I sleep through screaming alarms, neighbors, and babies.

Thirty-four police cars can roll into Oasis Springs, sirens howling, officers barking, I'm not flinching. Last summer a whole chopper landed on our roof. *It felt like an earthquake*, Munka swears. *Like the building was collapsing*. I slept like a baby.

Except now, I forgot how to sleep.

The harder I try, the tighter I squeeze my eyes, the further away sleep gets.

I've tried every trick—sheep counting, window opening, milk warming. Tonight, I took a long, hot shower until Dad shouted through the door, *Boy, I'm taking the water bill outta your allowance.*

To which I reply, *Umm, what allowance?*

I mean, I say it under my breath cuz I ain't stupid, but whatever.

I'm so desperate for sleep, I run through algebra equations in my head—and I know, you're all: *Major Nerd Alert! Yuck, Tony, who likes math?*

To which I reply: *Hol' up, hol' up, who said I LIKE math?! I'm just good at it.*

The point is, nothing works. I lost my superpower, and I may never sleep good again.

But okay, you want the capital-T Truth? Probably there's a part of me that *doesn't* wanna sleep, that's fighting sleep like it's a supervillain. Because that same part of me knows that nowadays sleep comes packaged with every flavor of bad dreams. The kind that scare you awake, your forehead and back soaked in cold sweat, your heart high-jumping outta your chest, you're almost choking to catch your breath.

And the other thing holding my sleep hostage?

Tomorrow.

Because tomorrow's maybe the most important day of my life.

# 2

*BOOM! BOOM! BOOM!*

I pop up in bed like, *Where's the fire, evacuate the building!*

It takes me a ten count to realize it's only Munka bang-ing down my door like a wannabe firefighter.

"Yo, *chill*." I yawn, de-crust my eyes. Thing about my sister? Munka's 100 percent chill-less. She stays at a ten— bossing me and Tasha like she's paying us a salary (FYI: she definitely isn't). At least three or four times a week, I gotta check her, remind her she's barely two years older than me.

*BOOM! BOOM! BOOM!*

Man, she for real right now? "Quit it! What do you want?"

"Less attitude for one," Munka snaps. "You're late, big-head!"

I'm about to fire back when my brain finally catches up with my eyes, I read the alarm clock, and—oh snap, she's right! I explode outta bed, grab my gear, and crash into the bathroom.

"Don't use all my hot water," Dad yells after me, like hot water's his favorite bottle of cologne that he's letting me borrow.

I brush. Wash. Pick my hair. Then deodorize so I don't gotta hear Munka's mouth saying I stink just cuz maybe I forgot to use it once or twice; as if rolling white pasty stuff that supposedly smells like "summer breeze" all over your armpits is the key to keeping the earth spinning right.

On my way to the kitchen, I pause outside my parents' room. The door's closed, and I can't tell if their light's on or not, if Mom's asleep or sitting in her chair next to the window, her finger tucked inside her latest library book, marking her page.

"Come in, Tony," Mom says without me knocking because, somehow, she always knows what I'm thinking. It's probably just one of those mom things, but it's kinda freaky.

The curtains are closed tight, but sunlight glows around the edge of the window frame. Mom's reading chair's empty; she's still in bed, wrapped in more blanket layers than a seven-layer burrito—even though it's way too hot in our house. She pops her head out of the covers like a butterfly busting outta its cocoon.

"You ready?" Mom says softly.

I shrug. "I don't know. I hope so. Maybe."

She smiles, more with her eyes than her lips. "You're ready," she says. "You got this."

"Thanks, Mom," I say, turning back toward the hallway.

"Tony?"

"Yeah?"

"You play ball because you love it, so no matter what happens today or any day, no one can take your love away because it's inside you, where it's safe. Okay?"

"Yeah, okay," I say back, even though I don't completely understand what she means. What I do know is, she's saying it because she loves me and that's enough.

In the kitchen, I fire off a text.

**To Terry**

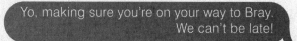

Yo, making sure you're on your way to Bray. We can't be late!

Then I'm dumping cereal into a plastic baggie and swaying my hips to the bachata bouncing through the wall from Ms. Martinez's place next door.

Tasha's bobbing her head to the beat and feeding her baby dolls at the table. "I don't care if you're not hungry. You're not leaving this table until you eat all your breakfast, y'all hear me?"

I laugh. "That sounds familiar," I say, sliding my fingers

across the bag's zip top. Why do they make these things so hard to close?

Tasha flexes her biceps. "You need milk today! Milk makes you strong!"

"You right," I tell her, gliding to the fridge and grabbing the jug. I toss my head back like I might howl, pour it straight into my mouth. Then, with my eyes still on the ceiling, I shake cereal into my mouth, Froot Loops rolling down my chin and T-shirt like an avalanche, Tasha cracking up like it's the funniest thing ever.

The way she's busting up right now, her brown-blond eyes glittering, her mouth wide like when the dentist says *say ahhh*—yeah, every day I used to scheme new ways to make her laugh like this, mostly stupid stuff I'd never do for anybody else, like pretending to mix up hot sauce for Kool-Aid and guzzling it so fast it ran down my chin, then shoving my head under the kitchen faucet, gulping cold water like my insides were on fire—because (1) Tasha has the best laugh ever. It's like her whole body's an erupting volcano. And (2) a few months back, I found out she was getting teased for being "chunky," and after I let those kids know that bullying my li'l sister—or anybody else—was a wrap, I also made it my mission to do whatever it takes to keep those crocodile tears away.

Except I've been slipping lately. I haven't felt funny for two weeks now.

"There, perfect," I tell her, wiping my mouth with the

back of my hand. She's still giggling as I slip a banana into my shorts pocket. "Be good."

"You be good," Tasha sings back. "And break your legs."

I laugh. "I think you mean *break a leg*, and thanks, Tash. I'll . . . try." I kiss her forehead, and then I'm rushing past an arms-folded, toe-tapping Munka.

"Boy, did you shower?" she yells with that same *you're guilty* voice the dude at the corner store shouts at us, *Only one of you allowed in here at a time* and *Let me see your pockets*, like anyone wants his stale junk.

Dad's in his green chair, lost in *Space Explorers*, his all-time favorite show.

Dad: TV's a waste of time. It obliterates your brain cells.

Also, Dad: the only thing I'm doing Saturday mornings is watching these aliens zip through the galaxy.

Normally, I watch with him. He doesn't ask me. I just slide onto the floor, careful not to block his view, scoot a little behind him so I can watch his face, too, and I don't say a word the whole show. I like it, too, but mostly I like that Dad likes it.

That it makes him forget stuff, like:

All the hours he's gotta work.

That his back hurts from throwing heavy boxes onto trucks at UPS.

That he's gotta be serious all the time. And strong. And hard.

That he thinks I'm too sensitive. Too emotional.

17

I like that it makes him happy. Sometimes he even smiles and laughs. And that makes me smile and laugh, too. Watching *Space Explorers* is when I like Dad the most—when he feels the closest to me, even though we don't talk. Like maybe for those couple of hours we understand each other.

"Yeah, *Mom*. Last night before bed," I call back as I skip past the slow-as-old-honey elevator, tearing down the stairs, until my sneakers hit the first floor.

Until I hit daylight.

# 3

Whoever named Oasis Springs has a wild imagination.

That, or they're mad positive. Like, you could shout, *Hey, your car's on fire!* And they'd be all, *Oh, fuuun, a bonfire, who wants s'mores?*

Don't misunderstand me—this is home. Maybe it's not for everybody, but I can't imagine living anywhere else. And I'm definitely not letting anyone talk trash about it.

But yeah, no one's clocking OS's five identical towers—a quintuplet of brownish-gray concrete buildings staggered in a circle—and thinking, *Ooohhh, an oasis!*

And as for the *Springs* part? Maaan, I got no clue.

There are exactly *zero* babbling brooks running through OS.

There is, however, an impressive collection of old mattresses tossed around the Jungle—our nickname for the abandoned, wildly overgrown parking lot behind C Tower. All us OS kids bounced on them like trampolines, until somebody's granddad shut it down.

But yeah, the only springs in Oasis Springs? They're rusting inside those old mattresses.

The way OS is set up, the court's in the middle of everything, so if you wanna get anywhere fast you cut across. We're fifty yards out when I spot leftover police tape wrapped around the north hoop, rippling in the wind like a kite tail.

"*Tony.*" Munka says my name hard, like when someone's on another planet and you're trying to get their attention. "I asked if you're nervous."

The four days they shut down the court to "investigate the shooting" were sunny and seventy degrees—perfect for balling. Not that weather meant anything. Before they shot D, didn't matter if the windchill was -37 degrees, there was always somebody on the court. But now—now it's ten days since it reopened and the only person putting up shots is a ghost.

I shake my head. "I'm cool."

Except the closer we get to the court, the more my feet and stomach are like, *Nah, not today, not yet,* so I steer us the longer, more scenic way outta OS instead. We squeeze single file through Stay-Out Alley, then pick our way through the

Jungle, its king and queen mattresses stained sunlight-gold.

"Because you have nothing to be nervous about," Munka says. "You got this, you know that, right?"

I shrug. It's weird, Munka being nice to me. Is it strange that I kinda *don't* like it? Seriously, ever since that night, the whole world's flipped inside out. Nothing makes sense. I don't have much, but I'd trade everything for life to be normal again. It's like the world's rocking a Snapchat filter—everything and nothing's changed at the same time. All I want is the way things were. How they're s'posed to be.

"Nuh-uh. None of that *I don't know* stuff. There are no *maybe*s inside that gym. You gotta *know* you got this the way you knew three weeks ago, when I couldn't pay you to stop talking about making this team. *I feel it in my bones*, you said."

The Walk sign snaps on, but Munka blocks me with her arm. "Look," she says. "I know things are . . . different now. But that feeling's still inside you, Tony. It's still in those way-too-skinny bones." Her voice sounds like a smile.

I shake my head. "But what if you're wrong?"

Munka never answers, because someone behind us shouts, "Yo, Tony!"

Suddenly, Munka and I are in perfect sync—we swivel around, peep who it is, and eye-roll at the same time.

The voice gets closer. "Tony, what's the word? Where you headed?"

I shake my head. *Not this dude again.* "We just out, man."

"C'mon, don't give me that. You're going *somewhere*. It's some kind of secret?"

I count backward from ten, like Ms. Maxwell said to do whenever my stomach starts knotting up. I take a deep breath. The knots are still there. "Tryouts."

"Oh, wait, today's the big day, right?" The voice is louder now, sharper. "Tony, why you walking so fast, man? I'm trying to ask you something. Slow up."

Officer Barrows revs the engine, and now his police car's creeping up the street beside me. One hand gripping the wheel, he leans across the front passenger seat to talk to us through the rolled-down window.

"Hop in, I'll shoot you two over to the Bray Center," Officer Barrows says, frowning as he realized his terrible choice of words.

Now my stomach's got more knots than the cords behind our TV. Not even playing, if it gets any tighter, I'm donating cereal chunks to this sidewalk.

"We're good, thanks. Have a nice day," Munka says, tacking on a fake smile.

"Tone, you gonna be at that town hall thing tonight? Cuz if so, I'll see you there."

I don't say a word. I don't nod when his window rolls up or wave when he speeds down the road, barreling through the intersection, ignoring the stop sign.

It takes more concentration than a game-winning free throw not to double over.

Because I forgot bad dreams don't need sleep to mess up your head.

Because daydreams work just fine.

Because the last time I saw Officer Barrows?

He was kneeling near center court, his energy like an exclamation point as he yelled into his walkie-talkie, *We need an ambulance now, shots fired, suspect down. I repeat, shots fired*, his fingers interlaced as he starts CPR, while his partner, Officer Sammy Truman—the shooter—stood so quiet and still you could've mistaken him for a statue. Or maybe a mime. Anything but a cop.

# 4

If I wasn't in my feelings *before* I got to the Bray Center gym, I am now.

Apparently, every kid in Milwaukee is trying out for Coach James's AAU team, the Sabres.

A few faces I recognize right away.

This kid Johnny Wu, who's all legs and arms. J-Wu's got the kind of nice all-around game that'll fill up a stat sheet quick—grabbing rebounds in heavy traffic, creating havoc on defense, dude goes hard. He never backs down. Every good team needs a J-Wu.

Then there's DJ Atkinson. He's from OS, too. Lives in A Tower with his granddad. Folks sleep on DJ. They size him up—he's shorter like me, doesn't look all that strong, and isn't super athletic—and they're like, *Nah, he's not built for this.* Except on the court, nobody works harder than DJ. Bro basically sleeps in the gym—he's the dude who plays all day and still puts up two hundred jumpers *after* everyone's gone. Only thing about DJ is he makes *everything* a competition. Every. Thing. Last year in our computer skills class, he was like, *Hey, Tone, bet I type faster than you.* I say, *DJ, let's hit up the corner store*, and he's all, *Bet I beat you to the corner.* On and on and on.

I guess when people underestimate you your whole life, you feel like you're never done proving yourself.

I check my phone, still no text from Terry. I hit him again.

**To Terry**

> Where you at?? The gym is wild rn. Get here!!

"Bro, you better put that phone down and put some shots up," a voice I recognize instantly says. My boy Isaiah, aka Zay. Outside of D and Terry, Zay's the closest thing I've got to a friend. Except he lives almost an hour away—which might as well be a different galaxy, so I rarely see him. "Dude, you been hitting the weights," I say, jabbing him in the chest.

And he's all teeth. "You know it. Added some crazy post moves, too."

I scan the gym. "Hold up, you here without your mom?"

Zay sighs. "Bruh, you already know." He points to the upper bleachers, and there's Ms. Carter, with her iPad and briefcase as always. She spots us and waves hard, like she's trying to put out a fire.

I wave back. "I'm still trying figure out how she makes it to all your ball stuff *and* still has time to be a big-shot lawyer."

Zay laughs. "As you can see, she's big on *multitasking*." Zay's face drops a bit. "Hey, I didn't get a chance to catch you at the funeral, but, uh . . ."

I nod. "It's all good, man."

Zay frowns. "But it's not, really. I mean, I wasn't as close to Dante as you, but I can't even front, I'm still shook."

A loose basketball squirts in my direction, and I toss it back to its owner. "Yeah, well, I guess it's kinda—"

"Here I am!" a booming voice cuts in. "Now we ready to ball!"

"This fool," I say, smiling as I fist-bump Special K. Yep, like the cereal. Special K and I are in the same grade—but no one believes it because dude's voice is all bass. Plus, he's *got a whole mustache*!

Special K grins because he's always grinning. "Surprised y'all suckers showed up. My game got so good, Coach'll probably start me at all five spots, ha." That's the other thing Special K is known for—mad hyperbole. Which is a fancy way of saying dude exaggerates *everything*.

"Wait, why y'all looking like somebody stole your bike?" Special K asks, his eyes darting back and forth between me and Zay. And then answering his own question, he drops his head. "Dante, right? Man, that whole thing's way messed up."

Zay and I nod. "If Dante wasn't safe, none of us are," Zay adds.

The three of us start warming up, shooting free throws, running a rebounding drill—and some of those butterflies I'd been feeling start to fade.

Fifteen minutes later, Zay's like, "Yo, where'd everybody go?"

And I hadn't noticed, but most of the kids are now crowding around a side court, deeper in the Bray Center.

I put up one more free throw, and then the three of us make our way over, pushing through the crowd until we're at the front.

"Of course," I say.

Zay nods. "Who else would it be?"

On the court, an intense game of one-on-one is already in progress.

Marcus Meeks versus KO Douglass—easily the best two players in the county, maybe the whole state, now that D's . . . gone.

But their games are super opposite.

Meeks is calculating. Takes his time, surveys the court, studies his opponent, lets the game come to him. He's never flashy. All he cares about is making the right play every time. Basically, Meeks lives up to his last name. He's mad humble.

Then there's KO—who is, well, *not* humble.

KO's all style. Always sporting brand-new gear from Nike or Adidas. Always rocking a fresh cut, including his famous "flat-line" part his barber etches into the side of his fade. *Cuz fools die tryna check me*, he boasts. And okay, he's not *completely* wrong. Really, the only flaw in his game is he can't shoot from deep. In last year's playoffs, he couldn't hit a triple to save his mama's life. But if his shot's falling early, good luck stopping him. Outside of D, KO has the nicest handles I've ever seen. And he *knows* it. And he makes sure *you* know, too.

The way he's jawing at Meeks right now.

"Bruh, you couldn't guard me if you was a pair of clippers," KO says, palming the ball near Meeks's face, daring Meeks to reach.

But Meeks doesn't flinch. He's not gonna let KO bait him.

"Just play, man," Meeks grumbles.

KO brings the ball so close to Meeks's head, it's basically kissing his cheek. "You scared I'mma blast you?" KO turns to the crowd. "Ya'll, this dude's scared I'mma—"

But before KO gets the words out, Meeks swipes the ball and sails into the paint for an easy bucket. The gym goes wild, including Special K, who almost knocks me down, he's bouncing so hard.

"You know KO hates that," Zay says.

"Whatever, he got lucky," KO says, waving off everyone's

laughs and jokes. "Bet he don't score again. Bet he—"

*Whroot! Whroot!* The whistle shrieks, and the gym quiets, all eyes on Coach James.

"Any of you wanna play real ball, I suggest you hurry over here now."

And we do.

Even KO, who selectively hustles—*bruh, I'm not tryna sweat in my new sweat suit*—jogs over.

Because even though everyone loves Coach James, everyone also knows that Coach doesn't play. When he says *jump*, you better already be in the air.

*Whroot! Whroot!* Coach blows that whistle again, and the kids closest to him cover their ears. "Let's go! Unless ya'll wanna do laps *before* we even start." Coach claps hard, the way he does when he's excited—which is always. For real, Coach can't keep still. He stays in motion—pacing the sideline, pumping his fists, stomping his feet, waving you over, waving you away. I bet money if Coach ever stops moving, he'll implode.

"We all know why we're here," Coach says, his eyes scanning every face in front of him. "But first, I thought we'd pause to honor one of our own. Dante Jones wasn't just one of the best ball players this team, this city, this country has ever seen . . . no, he was one of the best human beings to ever walk this planet. His heart was bigger than every court combined, and I know we all miss him. So, let's observe a moment of silence to remember our fallen brother and what he meant to us and to this community."

A few guys nod, a few say D's name aloud before bowing their heads . . . but me? My eyes drift upward, where two wide banners hang from the rafters, both embroidered with the same three magic words: AAU National Champions.

And below that, the names of the twelve kids who helped win it all. I've studied the banners enough times, I know just where to look: first column, third name from the bottom: D. Jones, #3.

Two national titles means the Sabres finished consecutive seasons as the number-one-ranked AAU team in the entire country. That's the thing about AAU ball—it doesn't matter how much talent you have, or who your coach is, or who's sponsoring your team—in the end, you're only as good as your national ranking. To be real, if anyone says they don't care if or where their team's ranked, it probably means they're not.

But if your goals are to—

Make it to the AAU championship game in Orlando, Florida.

Put your city on the map.

Make sure every player grabs a scholarship—either at one of the better private high schools, or maybe a parochial, putting you on the best possible path to eventually landing a Division I college or university scholarship.

Then you most definitely care. You care a whole lot.

At no point in three seasons were Dante's AAU teams

ranked lower than number six—which means for us new Sabres, there's even more pressure to not only win, but to win big.

To be real, it's wild that the Sabres won back-to-back AAU titles, especially since the team's only existed for three seasons. Most teams, even the ones that have been around forever, rarely sniff the playoffs, let alone bring home *one* chip—but then again, those teams weren't coached by future NBA Hall of Famer Hunter James or led by five-star recruit Dante Jones.

As if reading my mind, Coach points at the high gym ceiling, but beyond the championship banners, to D's Sabre jersey that now hangs beside them, his #3 retired forever. To D's two tournament MVP banners that sway gently in the air-conditioner breeze. "We all know what kind of player Dante was. I had the pleasure of coaching him on the high school team and in our AAU program, and you know what the most impressive thing I've ever seen that kid do out of all the mesmerizing things he did?" Coach pauses, his eyes brightening for a moment. "He treated everyone the same. No matter if you were the last bench player, or the equipment manager, or a parent, or a referee, or a scout, or a little kid, or an opposing player on our rival team, he never changed. He played the same way. He acted the same way. Of all the ways he was special, the way he loved people ranks way up there."

Coach clears his throat. "I'll be honest, there was part of

me that wasn't sure if I should coach this year. I wondered if we'd be better off focusing all our attention on doing something that would make a real difference." Coach surveys the gym like he's taking attendance. "But then I asked myself what Dante would want, and well, I think we all know what he'd say, yeah?"

More head nods along with mumbled yeses.

"As you all know by now, one big change I did make is I've turned over the seventeen-and-under coaching duties to Coach Aaron. They'll practice over at South Rec. Coach Aaron's been with me since we formed the Sabres, and I know those boys are in great hands. As for me, I'll be coaching a whole new squad, our fourteen-and-under team. Now before we begin, I want you to know that although some of you aren't gonna make this team"—Coach wags his head—"let's keep it real . . . *most* of you, I still appreciate you being here and showing up on time and I—"

The men's locker room door squeals open, breaking Coach's sentence in half like a pretzel stick. Everyone turns to see who it is.

"Uh-oh, Coach about to light into somebody," Special K mutters under his breath.

That's when Terry Jones strolls in, his backpack on both shoulders, his black Adidas slides squeaking across the shiny gym floor. Coach's eyes follow Terry as he slips into the back of the crowd like he didn't just interrupt everything. Everyone's eyes dart back and forth between

Terry and Coach, waiting for either one to say something. Normally, Coach would've been all over Terry—or any of us—but instead he only clears his throat and restarts like nothing happened.

"As I was saying, I appreciate you being *on time*. And I appreciate your effort. Your energy. Your commitment. And whether you make the team or not, you all know you can always come talk to me. My door's always open. Anytime. Anyplace. About anything. We good?"

"Yes, sir," everyone says, almost at the same time.

"We all know why we're here. We're looking for the twelve best players. Remember, it's not about how many points you score, or how good you look doing it. Be efficient. Affect every possession. Hold your own. Play team ball." Coach studies his clipboard. "Oh, and one more thing, I wanna introduce you to a member of my staff . . ."

Coach steps aside, making way for a Black girl sporting a jet-black ponytail, purple Lakers game shorts, and a clean white T-shirt that says *Ball Is Life*. Coach clears his throat. "This is Kiara James. She'll be recording our game film this season."

Kiara smiles, holds up a fancy black video camera. "Hi, guys. I'm also putting together highlight reels for every player on the team to help with your college recruiting."

Which is cool that Coach wants to do all he can to make sure we get into good colleges, but also it's kinda weird, right—that an under-fourteen AAU team is not only thinking about their players' college recruiting, but that there are college scouts watching twelve-, thirteen-, and fourteen-year-olds hoop, breaking down film, and projecting how good they think you can be. And if they thought you had it—like D did—actual college coaches came to your house, sat on your couch, and offered you a full scholarship to play ball . . . when you're still in middle school!

Umm, *and* she's rocking a pair of limited-edition black-and-gold *Black Mambas*. Who is this girl?

"And for those of you who haven't put it together yet, yes, this *is* my daughter. And you are to treat her with even more respect than you give me. Otherwise . . . well, you don't wanna know how that sentence ends, trust me."

Kiara shoots her dad the same look I throw at my parents whenever they're bugging, but Coach is already on to the next, and Kiara strolls back to the bottom bleachers. "All right, we're running five-on-five. Blue team is Isaiah Carter, Johnny Wu, Kenny 'Special K' Lucas, KO Douglass, and . . . Tony Washington. And they'll match up against Marcus Meeks, DJ Atkinson, Terry Jones . . ."

But after Terry's name, I don't even hear the second squad names, because all I know is Coach just called my name. I'm up now. This is my one shot to prove I belong out here. To make D proud. I can't blow it.

Dante's voice pops into my head—*You got this, Tone. Everything you been doing, all the drills, all the practicing, breaking down game film, it's all been about this moment right here, right now.*

But what if I'm not good enough, D? What if I let you down and don't make the team?

*No matter what happens, you are good enough, Tone. But not because somebody else says so. Because you know so. What I always tell you? You gotta believe in you. You gotta trust that your best is enough.*

*And are you kidding me, man. Tone, you've never let me down. Not once.*

But that night . . . that night I . . .

*That night's not yours to carry. Your only focus better be on this game. Now get out there and bust those dudes up.*

And I run out onto the court to join my team.

Because D's right—I gotta trust in myself. I gotta believe.

But also, he's wrong—because I *can* let him down. I already did.

See, that night he got shot?

I was supposed to be there, too. And if I'd been there on time, D might still be here.

Terry, now rocking the new gold LeBrons, steps onto the court beside me. "You ain't answer my texts? You good?" I ask him. "You ready to play?"

He nods, but his eyes say different. Terry, the kid who's always joking around, who you can't pay to be serious, that kid's been missing for weeks now. And this kid standing in his place, the "Terry" in front of me, looks like he's never tried to smile.

"Well, good luck, T," I say, extending a fist bump.

"Good luck, bro," he says quietly, weakly tapping my fist.

And I force a smile even though my stomach's low-key doing bigger backflips than those Jungle mattresses ever saw. "Hopefully, we both make it."

He nods, wipes his sneaker bottoms clean, and gets ready to catch the tip. And it hits me. All the time I spent preparing for this moment, I never thought about this scenario. I'd always thought about *after* tryouts—with a proud D smiling mad hard when me and Terry learned we made the team, that we were teammates who were gonna battle *together* on the same court. But this . . . this is not that. This is way different. This is me and Terry matched up *against* each other. Which means, if we want any shot at making this team, I've gotta go right at Terry and Terry's gotta go right at me. No taking it easy cuz we're friends. No playing soft because neither of us wants to show up the other. We've gotta go hard. Otherwise, how's Coach gonna know we're ready to do whatever it takes?

I think about asking Terry, *How do you wanna play this?* but then the whistle blows and the ball's tossed in the air, and there's zero time to feel sorry for myself.

Or worry about me and Terry.

That's gotta wait.

Now we ball.

**5**

They win the tip.

Their big man back-taps the ball into Terry's hands—and I finally see a look I recognize in Terry's eyes. That *I'm gonna destroy you* grin. His *my jumper feels extra wet today* glow.

But it's cool. I *want* his A game because I'm gonna give it to him right back.

I'm in Terry's shorts all the way up the floor. When he pulls up, I keep a hand in his face so he can't get a clean look at the basket.

Even when he dishes the rock to someone else, I stay on him like Velcro. He runs full tilt crosscourt, I run, too.

He fades to the far corner, I fade right with him, like the shadow he never asked for. I grab him, snag his T-shirt, force him outta bounds anytime he's near the baseline, and I shoulder-bump him even when he's away from the ball and outta the play—because I want him to feel me. I want him to know this is how it's gonna be all game long.

See, I know Terry's game. His ballhandling is average. He's not grabbing a lot of rebounds or dishing out mad assists. Nope, Terry's out here for one reason:

He shoots lights out.

And his release is scary quick. You blink, and before you can react—*hand down, man down*—Terry's midair, the ball already gone. Plus, he's got range. With ease, he can pull up and hit from anywhere.

So if you're guarding him, you gotta stay after him. No, more like *attached* to him. You fight through every screen. You chase him everywhere. You grab, pull, hold—whatever you can get away with. And most importantly, you can't ever let up.

"Man, bro, you gonna foul me every play?" Terry asks, knocking my hand off his hip. "I don't even have the ball."

I put my hand back on his hip, and again he slaps it away. "I'm gonna do what I gotta do, same as you."

He smirks. "You're not winning this game, you know that, right?"

And then before I can answer, he takes a few hard steps to his left, and I move right with him. Except next thing I know, my jaw's hitting a wall and I'm crashing to the floor at the same time Terry's catching a pass and putting up his shot. I don't even need to look. I already know—*swish*. Shane, the kid who set the vicious screen stares down at me and laughs. I hop to my feet, like it's nothing, even though my jaw's throbbing, and I shout at my teammates, "Y'all tryna get me killed? Call out the picks!"

Now it's my turn to bring the ball up, and Terry, not a great defender, doesn't even bother to pressure me. I call for a screen of my own, except Terry slips it and stays with me. I call for another pick, and this time, before Terry can react, I curl around the screen—wait for my big man to cut to the rim and I hit him with the perfect pass in stride. I'm already clapping before the ball even hits the net. "That's all day," I bark. "No way y'all gonna stop that."

And it's true—the game goes back and forth. Terry connects on two more jumpers, one from deep, the other a mid-ranger off glass. He finishes the game with a solid seven points, except he took nine shots to get there.

Isaiah fist-bumps me as we walk off the court victorious. "You locked Terry down, bruh. What he go? Three for eight?"

"Three for nine," I correct him. "But who's counting?"

Isaiah laughs, his short locs shaking. "See, this is why I like playing with you."

I laugh, too. "Oh, I thought it was those fourteen points I fed you in the paint."

Isaiah smiles. "I mean, that helps."

"Thought so," I say, nudging him on his side.

"How many assists you had?"

I shrug, but Isaiah calls me out. "Bruh, don't act like you don't know."

I grin. "I lost track once it hit double digits."

"My man," Zay says with another fist bump.

"Don't feel yourself too hard, Tone. You left at least a half dozen more on the court," KO says, coming out of nowhere.

I shake my head. "Wait, what?"

"Dang, K, let the man have his shine."

But KO's not done. "No shade. But we all know the only reason you got off how you did was because you had me and Zay catching your weak passes."

Zay waves KO off. "C'mon, K, Tone hit you with that dime in the corner."

KO laughs. "My baby sister could've made that pass."

I take a step to KO, and he squares his shoulders like he's ready to throw hands.

But truth is, neither of us wants to fight. KO's too much of a pretty boy and me—well, I'm not really a throw-hands kinda dude on my best day. But that doesn't stop either one of us from getting in each other's faces.

"Dude, what's your problem?" I ask.

But Zay throws his long arms between us. "Whoa, easy, boys. We're all on the same team, remember?"

"For now," KO says, sneering as he turns to walk away.

"We'll see if it stays that way *after* tryouts."

And I shouldn't let him get to me. I can't let anyone take me outta my game, especially today. But I can't lie, if a genie in a lamp granted me three wishes, one would be for Dante to still be alive, one would be for Mom to feel better, and the last one—

That KO *doesn't* make this team.

Lucky for him, genies don't hang out in Oasis Springs.

A good screen is a point guard's best friend.

A good screen creates space from your defender. It buys you separation—and separation means choices.

You can drive all the way to the rack.

You can pull up for a floater in the paint.

Or throw a lob for a monster jam.

There's a million ways to play it—but the key is timing. Go too fast or too slow and you blow your advantage.

First play of our second game, I motion for Zay to set a screen. Except both of our defenders are extra aggressive and jump the screen, forcing me to stay back. So now I'm thinking, *Okay, I gotta turn the corner faster.*

So, we reset the play. Zay screens, and this time I dive around him before my defender can react. And as I turn the corner, it's like the clouds part and there's nothing but unprotected rim ahead. This is gonna be an easy two points.

Except that's when my soul nearly exits my body as—*Whroot!*—Coach blows his whistle hard. "Moving screen," he signals. "Ball goes to red."

I shake my head. "C'mon, Coach, he was set."

But Coach is already on to the next play.

KO groans. "Turnover in the first fifteen seconds of the game. You for real?"

But Zay waves KO off, taps his chest. "That's on me, too." He nudges me with his shoulder. "We good, bruh. Brush that off, and let's get this W."

"Let's goooo," Special K adds, smiling.

I nod and drop into my defensive stance. *You made a mistake, Tony. Put it behind you and play your game.*

I D up my man, DJ, and he fends me off with his forearm. "Bet if you play me tight like you did Terry, I'mma feast in the paint all game."

I don't even reply. I just smile and flash him my *I'm about to lock you all the way down* look.

They inbound the ball, and DJ's dribbling between his legs, using his hips to keep me from stealing the ball. I play him tight up the court, crouched in my defensive stance, sliding, moving my feet. But his ballhandling's legit, so even with my pestering, he crosses half-court with ease, already calling for his center to screen me—the same play I ran and failed. Except when his big man plants on my left, I bark at Special K to *stay home, stay home*—meaning, don't switch guys, stay with your man and I'll stay with mine. Basketball's like math—it's all about playing angles. But again, just to be clear, am I good at math? Yes. Do I like math? C'mon, stop it. My math teachers don't even like math.

I slip the screen, tailing DJ like I'm his shadow.

I reach in and poke the ball outta DJ's hands. Special K scoops it and takes off dribbling the other way, now we've got numbers, a two-on-one fast break. Except somehow I trip over my own feet just as Special K tosses a bounce pass, and the ball sails out of bounds.

"Snap," Special K shouts. "Bro, you gotta get that."

I tap my chest. "That's all me. That's my bad."

I finish the game with more turnovers (5) than assists (4). I tell myself it's only the second game, but the rest of the games aren't *that* much better. I mean, yeah, there are a few moments where I look like I belong, including a game-winning no-look assist to KO in our fifth and final game.

But did I do enough to make the team?

Can't even call it.

I'm on the sideline, watching Terry's last game.

T's had a good day, and he's saved his best for last. He's annihilating his man with every brand of jumper—spot-up, catch-and-shoot, stepback, off-the-dribble. Might as well award him Perfect Attendance, Terry's not missing.

I smile as his defender bites hard on a fake, Terry breaking the other way. "Help! Help!" the defender shouts to his teammates, but Terry's already in flight as he flings another dagger three ball.

"Ball game," Terry announces, taking a bow. Actually, taking *four* bows in all four directions right at center court. Everyone's laughing, except for the dude who T just beat.

No, he's too busy bull-rushing T. He shoves T with the kind of energy you use to rocket someone to the moon.

But Terry doesn't sail far, luckily stumbling into a teammate strong enough to keep Terry upright.

"Okay, let's see your game *off* the court, bruh," the bull rusher says. Terry pushes him back, but the other kid barely moves. "That's it? Yo, you trash, man. Just like your trash brother."

And then in a flash, Terry's on top of the kid, throwing blurry punches. I try to yank Terry back, but he swings harder, faster. "Terry, that's enough, man!" But it's not enough for him.

Every punch a question and an answer, Terry keeps swinging. Doesn't even stop when he elbows me in the jaw, and I stagger backward, dizzy.

"Yo, you all right, Tone," Zay asks me, trying to check my jaw, except my hands are in the way. I wince but nod. "Yeah, I'm cool. But Terry . . ."

"Say less," Zay says. He walks over and wraps up Terry by the arms, Terry shouting to let him go and trying to squirm his way outta Zay's grip. But Zay's not letting go. And you'd think, okay, fight over. Except the other dude is the kind of punk who throws sucker punches, and he connects with a vicious uppercut on Terry's nose, blood squirting onto Terry's kicks, onto the gym floor.

"Dude, is you crazy?" Terry screams—except it's unclear if he's yelling at Zay for getting him punched or at the dude who threw the punch. Maybe he's yelling at me for trying to break it up. Maybe he's yelling at himself because he knows this isn't who he is.

And now he's shouting at all three of us, "You must be out your mind!"

And Terry, his nose still gushing blood, is lunging at the other dude, desperate to resume the fight when—*Whroot!* That whistle blows.

"What's going on here?" Coach James says, suddenly standing in the middle of the crowd. "Both of you out of my gym now."

I shake my head. "But, Coach, it's not Terry's fault. That dude started it. Terry was just defending himself."

But Coach isn't trying to hear that. "You know the rules. You fight, you're out."

The other dude's already walking away, waving at Coach like he couldn't care less about making the team, or what Coach thinks of him. But Terry stands his ground, his eyes locked on Coach, both hands still balled like fists.

"Terry, you too. Get outta here."

But Terry doesn't budge.

Coach shakes his head. "Terry, what you waiting for? You got something to say?"

Terry takes a step toward Coach. "Yeah, I got—"

I grab Terry's arm to pull him back, but he yanks away.

"This is stupid," Terry says to Coach. To all of us. "This whole thing doesn't even matter. Y'all know that, right? You think it's gonna change your life making this wack team? You think this dude actually cares about you? If you do, you're bigger idiots than I thought. For real, if y'all think anyone here cares about anyone but themselves, you playing yourself."

"Terry, *enough*. Go wait in my office," Coach says.

"You ain't my dad, man. I'm not waiting for you any-where."

"Terry, I know you're hurting," Coach says. "But that—"

"Not another person telling me how I feel," Terry says, his words cutting through Coach's sharper than D knifing through the lane for a layup.

Coach wags his head. "That's not what I—"

"You don't know me. You don't know what I'm feeling. You don't know anything. What, you think just cuz you coached my brother for a few years, that means you and me are auto cool, too?"

This time Coach doesn't reply. He stands there, his eyes locked on Terry's, doesn't even open his mouth, like he knows the best thing he can do is let Terry vent. I think about something D used to say: *You can't fix your game over-night.* Meaning, if there was something broken in your game, like maybe your left hand was weak, you could work on it all day, and yeah, you'd see improvement but the only way you were gonna take it to the next level was to prac-tice and work hard—because doing things the right way takes time. Maybe Coach knows that, too. That whatever's happening inside Terry, it's not something you can fix with a conversation, or a few encouraging words. No, if Terry was gonna get right again, it was gonna take time.

Terry turns toward the rest of us, like how on those TV shows a lawyer will turn away from the witness on the stand to work the jury. "What you thought, you was gonna switch things up this season, come through riding your white horse and save all us middle school hood urchins, huh? Maybe make yourself feel better, too, right?" Terry wags his head. "But lemme ask you something, *Coach*. How you gon' save all of us, *any* of us, when you couldn't even save D?"

"*Terry* . . . if you want to be on this—" Coach says, his voice sharp.

"Yo, *bump* you and *bump* this whole janky team. I'm out," Terry snaps, pivoting toward me. "You coming, Tone? Or you gonna waste your time with these fools?"

I rapid-fire four or five texts to Terry, but he leaves me unread.

I find Munka outside the Bray, jumping in the grass with the rest of her Fear Squad. My bad, *cheer* squad. School doesn't start for another two months, but you wouldn't know it, how hard Munka's been pushing her teammates. And I'd never tell her because if her head gets any bigger she'll sail to Jupiter, but I respect her hustle. Her focus. Before Munka, there was no cheer squad at our school. *It's not a priority*, everyone told her. *We don't have the resources,* the school board told her. But thing about Munka? When she wants something, she goes after it. And the more you tell her no, the harder she goes.

Munka snaps off the music. "Okay, everybody, way to grind today. Don't forget, we'll be here three days a week, *every* week, until school starts."

A hand shoots up. This girl Destiny who Munka can't stand. *If she cared as much about the squad as she does chasing girls, she'd dominate.* "Yes, Destiny?" Munka says, already shaking her head.

"What if we can only make it one day a week?" Destiny says, twirling her hair and blowing her gum into a pink bubble.

Munka laughs. "Girl, if you wanna be on the squad, I think you already know the answer."

Destiny frowns, her mouth fixed like maybe she wants to say something, but Munka's already pivoting toward me, her eyes bright with anticipation. Even before the words leave Munka's mouth, I already know what she's gonna ask.

"So, did you make the team?"

8

I see that sunflower suitcase on Mom and Dad's bed, and I already know this isn't gonna be one of those afternoons where Mom's flinging questions at me like we're in a water balloon fight and I'm all out of ammo. Normally, she'd tackle me soon as I step through the door, like:

*My favorite son, tell me, how were tryouts? You got a good feeling? I know you played better than you think. You're too hard on yourself, Tone. I wish you could see you the way I see you.*

But that sunflower suitcase means we're not talking try-outs tonight. Which is sorta a relief—it's the last thing I wanna think about right now. Except I wish there was a better reason why tonight's different.

I like to think of it as Mom lives two types of days.

There are Good Days.

On Good Days, Mom is the most awesome human alive.

Good Days she's singing all day around the house, while she's folding clothes—her least favorite thing in the world to do—while she's cooking dinner, even while she's sorting through the bills. Those days nothing can touch her. Nothing can make her sad. Those days are the days you show her your bad grade on your science test, and yeah, she'd still shake her head, tell you that school isn't something you play around with, that you better get that grade up quick before report card time comes around—but that was it. No dish duty for a month. No scrubbing the tub every weekend. No privileges taken away.

On Good Days, she has the best laugh.

On Good Days, she surprises you with random hugs that at first you pretend to resist because c'mon, you're too old—but man, if those hugs don't warm you from the outside in.

But then there are Other Days.

On Other Days, she's still the most awesome human in the world but just differently, in ways hard to explain.

You know it's an Other Day when the sunlight or one of your sisters wakes you up instead of Mom smiling down at you from the edge of your bed, her mouth always spitting the same three words: *How'd you sleep?*

You know it's an Other Day when you walk past Mom's room and her bedroom door's closed tight and there ain't nothing but darkness down there at the bottom edge of the door, where usually light escapes. You know it's an Other Day when you have to pack your own lunch for school and because you woke up late you don't have time to get the right ratio of peanut butter to jelly, and you definitely don't have time to carefully cut off the nasty crust the way Mom always does so perfectly.

You come home, and there are two possibilities for an Other Day:

1. She's still in her room, not one thing in the entire house different than how it was when you left out that morning.

Or 2. She's sitting silently at the kitchen table, a half-eaten piece of fruit in front of her, maybe a banana or a cup of yogurt with only one spoonful missing—just enough food to help Mom swallow her daily medication. She tries to smile at you, but she can barely get her smile muscles to twitch on an Other Day.

Sometimes when the Other Days turn to Other Weeks, a small suitcase will appear one morning, empty and open at the foot of Mom and Dad's bed.

By the end of the day, it'll be three-quarters filled and you'll carry it to the front door and down the building steps and out into the sun or rain or snow. You lift it as high as your head and settle it in the back of the family mini-van. You pull Mom in for a hug, and she tries to warm you up; she wraps her arms around you with the same intensity as on the Good Days, but nothing doing—you both stay colder than the middle of a freezer.

She tells you how much she loves each of you, and you group-hug her until Dad breaks it up and climbs into the driver's seat, Mom sliding into the seat next to him. She smiles like it hurts. Like she's just had tooth surgery or come in from the coldest blizzard.

On this kind of Other Day you wave Mom goodbye until you can't see the van's taillights anymore, until the only thing you have left is a sore arm.

On that kind of Other Day, Dad comes home a few hours later, alone, the suitcase gone. *Mom just needs some rest*, he always explains. *It's not about you or me or us, you understand?* And you want to understand, but you don't—not really. But you nod anyway, and you hear the words leap outta your mouth as if you were some ventriloquist's dummy—*Yeah, I understand*, you say. *We're okay. Everything's okay. Mom just needs rest.*

Normally, I spot all the Other Day signs, but this morning, I was so focused on getting to tryouts, I missed them.

Dad opens and closes every kitchen cabinet, and Munka reads his mind. "She didn't get to the grocery store this week," she tells him quietly, like she doesn't wanna say it, like Mom's one of us kids and Munka's breaking the *don't rat on each other* code.

Dad's eyes are red, and he keeps rubbing the top of his head like how he does when he's ready to fall into his mattress.

Dad sighs. "Y'all want pizza?" he asks. And honestly, we're sick of pizza, but we know Dad's doing his best right now, so we're all, *Yeah, that's cool.* Except we're not convincing enough, because Dad opens the fridge again, riffles through the pullout drawers like maybe he missed something, like this is all a magic trick and this time there's gonna be smothered porkchops and mashed potatoes and gravy and corn on the cob inside, waiting.

Tasha tugs on his joggers. "Daddy, you tired? You look too tired. You want me to cook you some cereal or Toaster Struttle?" she asks. Her way of saying *strudel.*

Dad smiles, rubs her head, her barrettes bouncing in her pigtails. "That's so nice of you to ask, baby girl, but I'm okay. I'm never too tired to put some food in your belly, yeah?"

Tasha nods slowly, her head dropping toward the floor. Dad lifts her in the air, whirls her around in the middle of the kitchen. And she's squealing, "Faster, Daddy, faster!" And I remember when I was that small, when it was me spinning round and round knocking stuff off the counter, when my questions never made Dad more angry or more frustrated or sad.

When Dad first started working his second job, he'd come home in between and watch *SportsCenter* sitting in his living room chair because he was afraid if he lay down, he might not wake back up. And I'd say, *Dad, you tired? If you're tired, why don't you go lie down? I'll make sure you get up.*

But he'd always force his eyes cartoon-big like when they're bugging outta your head—and he'd say, *Ain't nobody tired, who looks tired?* And then he'd be snoring two minutes later. I haven't asked him if he's tired in a long time. Maybe because I know the answer.

The last time I asked, he shook his head and said, *I stay tired, man, but it's okay. It's a good tired. It's that* taking care of your family *tired. And if you gotta be tired, there's no better reason than that.*

Dad swings Tasha my way, her feet nearly smack me in the face, but I jump back. "Whoa! Easy!" I snap. Okay, maybe I didn't need to jump, but still—in this house, if I want anybody to notice me, I gotta make everything bigger than it really is.

But Dad ignores me, swings Tasha up onto his shoulders, and now Tasha's playing with Dad's hair and Dad's smiling like it's his fave game.

"Dad? Pizza?" I ask. "Want me to order?"

"Daddy, I don't want pizza," Tasha says, twisting a clump of Dad's thick hair.

Dad sighs now—but if I'd said that, he woulda lectured me for two hours on being content with what we got, that lots of kids would kill for what I got—to which I *wanna* reply, *They don't have to kill for it, they can just have it.* But I'm not stupid, so I keep my mouth shut.

"Know what? I don't want pizza, either," Dad says, rubbing the skin above his eyes like it's a gold lamp, like he wishes he had a genie, too, and he says the words I know he hates the most, the words I love—

"Pack your bags for Big Mama's."

"But the rally," Munka says, looking up from her phone.

"You know your grandma's not missing that rally, either," Dad says.

"Big Mama doesn't miss anything," Tasha says, transferring a barrette from her own hair onto Dad's.

"Right," Munka says. "That's the problem."

# 9

I've never been to a rally.

I can't even tell you what a rally is.

All I know is the entire neighborhood's packed inside the community center because tonight we find out what happens to Officer Truman—aka the cop who killed D.

"Wow, all these people from OS?" I ask Munka as Dad leads us three kids through the maze of people and folding chairs. We got here fifteen minutes ago, but we still haven't found seats because people keeping popping up out of nowhere and talking to Dad—like I didn't think my dad even knew this many people.

Munka shrugs. "When something pops off in OS,

everybody got something to say about it. It's like family business."

Everyone says that about OS. That we're all family, whether you like it or not.

Like Ms. Ross, who lived in the apartment across from us—anytime she knew Mom was gone or not feeling well, Ms. Ross always "accidentally" made too much oxtail stew or "accidentally" bought more bread and milk than she could use.

And when Ms. Ross needed hip surgery, only her insurance wouldn't cover the wheeled walker or any of the dressings and bandages, Mom "accidentally" bought all of it and "accidentally" left it outside Ms. Ross's door.

Thing about a place like OS, people assume just cuz you live in close quarters that everybody is probably being nosy and up in everyone else's business—

And yeah, sure, people like Mr. Otis definitely love talking about *the loud fight over in C3 last night because he came home at two in the morning again* or *the Turner boy over in D2 who's back in the hospital because he can't stop being sad*—and Miss Peach, who is always asking mad personal questions that don't have anything to do with her like *Heard your dad is still claiming he's innocent, that he could've already been out if he'd take the deal they offered him, well, is that true?*—but honestly, it's not like folks like Mr. Otis and Miss Peach are that bad, either.

Think about it: Miss Peach's real name is actually Miss

Holloway, but because she's steady propping against everyone's door brown paper bags filled to the top with so many peaches that one or two inevitably spill out and roll across the floor, some floors looking like you were in a peach orchard instead of an OS tower, everybody knows her as Miss Peach.

People call you a name like that, how bad can you be?

Point is, I shouldn't be *surprised* that the whole community shown up here today—OS folks have always done this. But I've never seen so many of us together at the same time.

This is maybe three hundred people crowded into a space meant for half that.

This is three hundred voices all talking at once.

This is three hundred bodies buzzing with anger and hurt and sadness.

This is different than anything I've ever seen or felt.


I wave until Big Mama spots me.

Her eyes brighten, her Mary Poppins purse whacking everybody in the head as she weaves through the commotion. A few folks turn around upset, like they ready to throw hands, but when they see it's Big Mama, their faces fall into smiles. Everybody loves Big Mama. She squeezes down our row and takes the saved seat between me and Tasha.

She zerberts Tasha on the cheek. Wraps me in a bear hug. "How are my favorite people in the world doing? I missed you so much."

"We missed you, too," I tell her.

Munka leans forward in her seat and floats her an air kiss, but Big Mama's not having it. "Nuh-uh, girl. You better get your behind over here and greet me right."

If you know Munka, you can tell she wants to complain, or at least sigh, but she moves past Tasha and hugs Big Mama. "Now, that's better, baby. You doing okay?"

Munka nods. "Yes, ma'am."

"Good," Big Mama says. She clears her throat until Dad turns toward her. He grins. "Hey, Mama. How you doing?"

"A lot better now that I'm surrounded by my grandbabies. At least somebody loves me around here."

Dad shakes his head. "Okay, Mama. This really ain't the time or the place for—"

Big Mama cuts Dad off. "You really about to tell the woman who pushed your big head outta her belly what the time or place anything's for?"

Dad holds up his hands in surrender. "Good to see you, Mama. I'm glad you're here."

"Mmm-hmm," she says, already whirling back to me and Tasha.

Once upon a time, Munka loved Big Mama as much as us—and deep down she still does. Only thing is Big Mama doesn't understand why Munka spends so much time on IG and Twitter complaining about which of her friends liked this or ignored that. *If it makes you so upset, why not put down your phone?* Big Mama likes to say. It's not that Big Mama's super against social media. *I just don't like that it makes us care too much about what other people think about us. As long as you're not hurting anyone, do what makes you happy.*

To which Munka replies: *Doesn't that mean I shouldn't care what you think?*

Except she never actually says that *to* Big Mama; Munka's annoying but ain't crazy!

"Tony, how was tryouts?" Big Mama's one of few, other than teachers and random old people, who only call me Tony, never Tone.

I nod. "It's like I either played really good or really bad. I don't know if I'm gonna . . ."

Big Mama squeezes my shoulder. "No matter what happens, the fact you still showed up when you had all the reason in the world to quit says a lot about the person you are, Tony. I'm proud of you. D's proud of you."

Two city council members, Police Commissioner Davis Pruitt and Mayor Lenora Wallace herself, sit behind a long table at the front of the room, each with a microphone and name card. Mayor Wallace leans into her mic:

"If everyone can find their seat, we're ready to begin," she says.

It's like in school when Principal Jackson tells everyone to *settle down* during assemblies—Mayor Wallace is all, *The sooner we're all settled, the sooner we can begin.*

"We're here today regarding the petition to have Officer

Sammy Truman removed from service and placed on imme-
diate probationary—"

"Nuh-uh," someone yells deep in the back. "Not proba-
tion! We want him fired!" It's a voice I recognize but don't
place right away. I crane my neck around trying to figure
out where the voice came from.

And that's when I see him—Terry, standing at the back
of the room, surrounded by five or six older OS kids. Kids
Mom's always warning me and Munka to avoid.

*I feel bad for those kids*, Mom said. *They're angry and confused, and they're just trying to survive. But that's not an excuse
to hurt other people.*

I guess I thought Mom meant they were bullies—I'd seen
them pushing kids around, demanding they come off their
new sneakers or phone or watch. Sometimes they messed
with older people, too.

Later I realized Mom was talking about the things they
did for the neighborhood drug dealers and corner boys—
running errands and holding "work" for them. That this
was you *hurt people*. What's Terry doing with those guys?

Terry and I meet eyes, but he quickly looks away.

"That cop for dang sure ain't coming back to OS," someone in the back cries out. "What happens when he shoots
another one of our kids?"

"How many of our kids gotta die before enough is
enough?"

Mayor Wallace clears her throat—*ahem*. She leans into

her mic until she's practically kissing it. "Yes, thank you, and your concerns will be heard, but for the sake of order, if we can limit the outburst to—"

"We're not gonna sit here and let you talk down to us. You're not about to pacify us with no talk about how *you hear us and you're gonna do what you can*. We're tired of that. We're done with that," Miss Peach says, popping up out of her seat near the front.

People explode in an applause so loud the mayor has to stand there, waiting for the noise to die down before she can reply.

The meeting goes like this for over two hours—which all that time, you might think that our concerns were heard. That a plan to make things right was set in motion.

But you'd be wrong—because even before the meeting started, the decision had already been made: not only does Officer Truman get to keep his job, he's gonna be officially back on the street as early as next week.

It seems everyone at the table has an excuse to justify this injustice:

*POLICE COMMISSIONER PRUITT: It's an isolated incident, and Officer Truman has an outstanding record of service in this community.*

*CITY COUNCILMAN TROY ATKINS: Policing is hard. Sadly, sometimes bad things happen to good people.*

*CITY COUNCILWOMAN TIFFANY JORDAN: We all want answers. We all want justice. But justice isn't assigning blame somewhere it doesn't belong.*

MAYOR WALLACE: *It's a tragedy of epic proportions. There's no way around it. Everyone at this table is sick at the loss that this community has suffered, that the Jones family has suffered. We understand your outrage. We sympathize with your pain and anguish . . . but as awful and as tragic as this incident is, at the end of the day, Officer Truman did his job. Should there be any future developments, we will carefully review any evidence to the contrary. In the meantime, we ask that we all do our part to bridge the divide between the police department and our community at large. No amount of looting, rioting, or bloodshed will bring back Dante Jones.*

After every statement, *Nooo* echoes around the cramped room.

People shout, *Are you kidding me? Are y'all out y'all minds?* People are angry. People cry. People scream. People wag their heads, say, *I knew this was gonna happen.* People shout, *You see, this is how they do us, you try to do things their way and this is what you get.* People wave their fists at the committee. People wave their fists at the sky. People curse, people cry into their hands and into other people's shoulders, people pray aloud. The same word—*injustice*—bounces everywhere like a Superball.

Dante's aunt Tracy collapses in her chair, people crowding around held back by a man yelling, *She needs air, y'all back up, give her space, she needs room to breathe,* while a woman in dark blue hospital scrubs makes sure Aunt Tracy's okay.

And no, I don't pass out, but everything's spinning, like a

giant hand reached down from the sky and spun the whole building like a top.

How can the people behind those mics be so smart but so stupid? How could they "investigate" the facts and decide the way Dante died was okay?

No one leaves after the meeting, until they flash the ceiling lights, and we all complain as we spill onto black grass in the silver-blue night.

Dad says, "It's a full moon. No wonder the world's gone crazy."

Except when I look up, the moon's ducked behind clouds—but still its soft gray light shines through, like when your hand covers your phone screen and your palm glows.

We split into three directions: the parking lot, the bus stop, or the sidewalk that eventually takes us home.

"Be right back," I call over my shoulder as I weave through the crowd, searching for Terry, even though I don't know what to say when I find him.

*Sorry your brother isn't getting the justice he deserves?*

*Sorry people keeping talking about his death like it's long in the past.*

*Like it's a thing to start forgetting.*

*But healing isn't forgetting.*

I spot him, just as I'm giving up, in the back seat of a large, all-black SUV, neon purple lights glowing underneath it, Terry's forehead pressed against the window glass, his eyes as dark as the center of your fist.

"Terry!" I yell as the SUV rumbles past me. "Terry!" I shout as the big truck speeds into the night.

And here's the thing that we're all thinking but aren't saying: if they killed Dante, maybe the brightest star Oasis Springs has ever seen, they won't think twice about killing us.

# 10

Leaving OS, it's like an episode of *Space Explorers*, and our old car is a spaceship hurtling the four of us into the dark toward some distant planet (Big Mama's), blasting through our old galaxy. I watch the laundromat that eats all our quarters every Saturday slide behind us. The corner store where Galatica the Cat hangs out, slinking up and down the three aisles like she's the manager. Then we pass Abe's Barbershop and Tri-America Bank, also known as the building Dad always comes out of mumbling, *It's like there's a hole in our bank account.* Finally, we zip past Omar's Deli, which isn't much to look at—Mom calls it a "hole-in-the-wall"—but everyone knows if you want the best sub sandwich, it's Omar's or forget about it.

And then Dad's turning onto the ramp for the highway, and *whoosh*, just like that, faster than warp drive, our old galaxy's slipped away.

It's weird: the older you get, the smaller the world feels.

I almost forget that Tasha's asleep on my shoulder.

Dad's listening to the baseball game on the radio.

Munka's nose is buried in her phone.

I fire Terry a text that I know he won't answer.

**To Terry**

> Bro, you okay?? You kicking it with those dudes now? Fr?

The closer we get to Big Mama's, the farther we are from home.

The farther we are from home, the more everything changes.

Goodbye, barely-on streetlamps and crumbling sidewalks.

Bye, squatty brown buildings.

Big Mama's house is redbrick with huge porch *and* a porch swing. The house sits on top of a small hill, and there's no driveway, so we park on the street.

Other things that are different:

There are zero towers.

There's more grass than concrete and trees in every yard.

And check this out: there are *yards*. Front yards, back-yards, even side yards.

Who even knew *side yards* was a thing?

*    *    *

All these bags, you'd think we were never going home.

I shoulder my duffel. Hand Tasha her small unicorn roller suitcase.

Then I'm lifting Munka's large duffel.

And Munka's overstuffed backpack.

And Munka's ginormous suitcase.

I feel like I say this all the time, but yo, is she for real? "You say you hate staying at Big Mama's, but you pack like you tryna live here forever."

"Bro, I'm helping you," Munka says, rolling her eyes. "This way, maybe you'll sprout half a muscle on those chopstick arms."

I eye-roll her right back. "Help less."

Dad sends us in first. "I need a minute," he mumbles, his hands still gripping the steering wheel. The only thing Dad dislikes more than spending time with Big Mama is *living* with Big Mama. They have one of those love-hate relationships—Big Mama *loves* to give Dad a hard time, and Dad *hates* every second of it. *Our relationship is . . . complicated*, Dad likes to say.

Me? I love kicking it at Big Mama's house.

Big Mama welcomes us with her booming voice, bear hugs, and the sweet air of . . .

My eyebrows slide up. "Big Mama, you baking?" I ask.

She winks. "Why? You don't like peach cobbler, do you?"

Tasha and I do our *we eating cobbler* dance, and Big

Mama cracks up. "You that happy for the cobbler, wait until you see what I got cooking for dinner." Big Mama turns to Munka. "Hi, Miss Munka. You gonna stand there ignoring your grandmother or . . . ?"

"We both know nobody can ignore you," Munka says, forcing her feet toward Big Mama, kissing her cheek the way you kiss a bear.

Big Mama has this whole big house all to herself, but it didn't used to be that way.

Dad grew up here, with his four older sisters.

Auntie Gloria. Auntie Marie. Auntie Sage. Auntie Layne.

Dad was a baby when Big Mama bought the house and they moved in.

Dad didn't tell me, though. Nope, Big Mama showed me the picture—she's cheesing real hard standing in the front yard next to the Sold sign, Auntie Gloria's posing with her hand on her hip like she's got an attitude, because she does, haha. Auntie Marie is grinning like Big Mama, except she's missing her front two teeth. Auntie Sage and Auntie Layne, the twins, are kneeling in front of Big Mama, looking like Big Mama made them take this picture and they can't wait until it's over. And Dad? Dad's wrapped in a yellow blanket, Big Mama cradling him in her arms. Dad says not much has changed, that everything is basically how it was when he was my age.

There's so much room. I mean, four bedrooms, *plus* a finished basement, *and* a mostly finished attic? Big Mama has enough space for an entire starting lineup—which is the total opposite at our house, where you can't breathe without hitting somebody with your chest.

Between my bedroom closet and the big dresser, I put away all my clothes, shooting my balled-up socks into the top drawer, nothing but net every time. I run my fingers on the back of the closet door where Dad—maybe when he was my age—carved his initials into the wood, small enough so that most people wouldn't even notice.

I shut the closet, close the drawer, and pick up the photo collage on the bedside table. It's pics of our family, the one I was born into and the one we've made.

The top of the dresser is covered in gold trophies and first-place ribbons—Dad's from his "basketball glory days," as Big Mama likes to call them. Apparently, Dad was pretty good—not D's level good—but he was the starting point guard for three years in high school and he hit the game-winning shot that won the state chip, earning him tournament MVP honors.

He played a little college ball, too, but he blew out his knee halfway through his first season, and according to Mom, Dad never stepped foot on another court ever again.

There are also lots of pics on the dresser. Pics of our parents' friends who we call auntie and uncle, pics with D and Terry and their aunt cheesing at one of Dad's world-famous BBQs, pics where we're smiling and laughing, pics on roller coasters and in bumper cars, pics where we're babies who fall asleep on Dad's chest, where we spit up on Big Mama's shoulder, where Mom's asleep on the floor next to our cribs, pics where all Mom's days are Good Days, where Dad's not dozing at dinner during his own prayer, pics where from our faces, light and brown and free, you'd think we never argued, you'd think we were nothing but happy. That we never ever worried about having enough.

Enough money. Enough time. Enough heat and air. Enough space and support.

But we got each other, which means we got love.

So much love, I can't see us ever running out, or even low.

No, we've got enough love for a hundred families.

And I wonder, if Mom knows we've got enough for all her Other Days combined?

That she's enough Mom, always. That one of her Best Days is worth four or five Other Days, easy.

And I wonder, as D's life seeped out onto the same concrete he dreamed upon, did he know he was loved? Did he feel peace, knowing he never took plays off, that he held nothing back? *Leave it all on the court*, he'd say. And he did. He left everything on the court.

How many times did D fall on that asphalt, stumbling on a fast break or boxing out for a rebound and losing his footing? Except every time he got up, dusted himself off, smiling as if he knew that falling only made him stronger, that losing his balance now meant he'd stay on his feet the next time. D rarely made the same mistake twice. *You good?* I'd ask and he'd grin. *Always,* he promised, *always.*

And it's easy to look at his death as a senseless loss. It's easy to say he broke his *always* promise. But maybe he knew that he'd live on in each of us.

In Terry. In his aunt. His neighbors and cousins and the guys that play chess under the corner-store awning as if it's their job. In me. In Tasha and Munka. In Coach.

I wouldn't put it past D. Because the one thing he taught me that'll I never forget is: *Never underestimate yourself. There are a lot of ways to affect a game. Little things that don't show up on the stat sheet. But those things are just as important.*

Right now feels just as important.

Any minute now and Coach will post a list with twelve names that together form a team.

I wanna be on that list more than I can explain.

And I want Terry on it, too.

I want it so bad.

Because D lives on inside us.

And he belongs on the court.

# 11

I can't make myself look—so I make Munka.

"Hit refresh again," I tell her. I'm doing that thing where you cover your eyes with your hands, but you're cheating, peeking between your fingers.

Because yeah, I wanna know, but also, I don't.

*Whatever*, it makes sense to me, ha.

"Boy, I swear if you don't stop hanging over my shoulder . . ." Munka says, twisting her face like those weird paintings Ms. Hall showed us in art, where the halves of a face don't match. I can't remember the artist, but I'm pretty sure dude got his ear chopped off—which sucks but also, if he had a big sister, lucky him. Maybe if I only had one ear, I'd only have to hear half of Munka's complaining.

I abandon her left shoulder to look over her right.

"Toooe Kneeeee, *don't*," she hisses, her face tighter than a jar of pickles. She's the Hallmark of faces; she's got one for every occasion.

"Foot, shoulder, stomach," I reply. Because when Munka's annoyed, she stretches my name into *Toeeee Kneeee*, like she's playing Quick, name a body part! So, I do. First few times I made this joke, she laughed, but nowadays it maybe gets a half smile.

I reach for her phone, but she jerks it away. "Boy, think I'm playing?" she whisper-yells.

Whisper-yells because Big Mama's in the kitchen humming her gospel hymns. All of 'em different but using the same words: *praise . . . deliverance . . . love.* If I gotta be honest, Big Mama's singing voice? Yeah, no one's putting her on *The Voice* anytime soon. Another reminder Mom's not here. Mom, whose voice could even make Quick, name a body part! sound beautiful.

She grits her teeth. "It's not even five thirty yet."

"Did I mention that this year's championship game is gonna be in Orlando, aka home to Disney World?"

"Only two dozen times, yeah. But listen," Munka says. "I'm waiting on an important text right now, so ask Big Mama to look for you, you that scared."

"One, ain't nobody scared. Two, staring at your phone isn't gonna make this *important* text come faster. And three, you already got the site pulled up."

Munka groans. "As soon as we check this list, you gotta go." She taps her phone, and instead of watching the screen, I watch her face. Her eyes rise and her cheeks fall. "Oh, snap. It's up," Munka shrieks. She aims the screen my way, but I push it back.

"No. You look."

She asks if I'm sure, but she's already scrolling down the page.

And I wait for it. For her face to turn happy and excited, or . . .

She shakes her head, forces her eyes to meet mine, like the way people looked at me at D's funeral—when there's nothing to say that means enough.

My sister reaches for me—her hand moving so slow a glacier would blow fingers outta the water in a race. Slow enough I can escape if I want. Slow enough I see the sharp white scar between her thumb and first finger, the day I got my training wheels off. *Don't hold on to me*, I told her, except the second she let go my brain forgot how to brake and my bike's moving too fast—*Munka! Muuunkaaa!* I'm yelling— and I'm headed for the intersection, I'm gonna roll right into traffic—but then Munka's flying beside me, throwing her arm into the back tire spokes, blood running down her arm, but there's not a single tear in Munka's eyes. She doesn't even look at her sliced hand, only asks if I'm okay.

Another thing I see: a message drawn in blue ink, one letter on each of her knuckles.

She does this sometimes, writes herself reminders on her fingers, her arms, her palms.

Today there's an *S* on her thumb.

On her first finger a *T*.

On her middle an *O*.

A thick *P* on her ring finger.

All four letters lined up perfectly with the black mole on her pinkie, like it's the period.

*STOP*, it says. But stop what? Her hand's now close enough to touch me, but I stumble backward outta her reach.

Because what Munka doesn't know is, I don't need her making me feel better because I don't feel anything inside.

Instead, I shrug like it's no big deal. A hard shrug, like *so what, who cares*. And I want to say those words, too—but the words won't leave my lips. I want to scream them outta me. Except they're trapped in my throat, and a match is struck, so now those words are on fire, every syllable burns, my words and tongue turning to ash, shrinking to nothing.

I smile. I look my big sis in her watery eyes, and I say: "Who even cares about a silly game throwing a stupid ball into a dumb net?"

And now both of her slow-moving hands are reaching for me.

And her other hand has another blue-inked word.

And her palms press into both of my cheeks like I'm a basketball she's getting a feel for.

This time I don't pull away or say, *Ugh, gross.*
This time she doesn't roll her eyes or call me *boy.*
*DON'T,* her right hand says.
And because my brain's dumb, I read: STOP. DON'T.
But I've got it backward.

Later, when I'm alone in bed, I pull up the Sabres' team
website on my phone.

What if Munka missed my name? What if Coach
uploaded the wrong list? Mistakes happen.

But no matter how many times I scroll, *Tony Washington*'s not on the list.

I tap refresh, but nope, nothing changes.

I keep refreshing until it's too hard to see because weird
water's falling from my eyes.

But relax, it's not what you think. I got onion juice on my
fingers from Big Mama's chili. There's an eyelash on my
eyeball. Dust particles are messing with my allergies.

Who would've thought that a list could hurt so bad?

I'm so caught up in my own defeat, I don't notice at first.

Not until I'm waiting for Munka to finish her three-hour pre-bedtime routine—which is more proof Munka's only posing as a human because only an alien with four hundred teeth would need three hours to floss, tell me I'm wrong.

Anyway, my phone's buzzing when Munka finally exits.

**From Zay**

Sorry, bro, you should've made it. Mom says so, too. Says she'll talk to Coach, but I told her wait until I talked to you.

Nah, everybody who made it deserves it. Just kick butt for me aiight??

I got you!!

I'm kinda tripping Terry made it after he went off. I get he's been through a lot but I've been on teams with negative energy and it sucks.

T will be cool. He's gonna figure it out.

And there's the silver lining I missed when I was too busy drowning in my feelings.

Terry made the team.

And no, not because Coach felt sorry for him, because (1) that's not how Coach moves and (2) if you watched Terry at tryouts, when he wasn't walking in late or fighting idiots, you know he earned this.

**To Terry**

CONGRATS!!!! You did it!!! So pumped for you!!

I told Coach I don't wanna play.

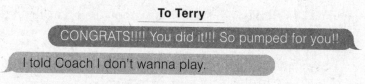

81

*　　*　　*

I knock louder.

Down the hallway, in another apartment, someone's laughing their whole butt off.

My stomach growls; the entire floor hallway smells like bacon.

Mom's face pops into my head, we're on opposite sides of our kitchen table, and she's pushing an ugly mountain of brussels sprouts my way—this maybe a month ago. But my nose scrunches, and I slide the plate back to her, like *hard pass*. But Mom always finds a way to win. *Tone*, she says, grinning, *everything's better with bacon. You don't believe me, wrap this table in bacon, see how many people start gnawing wood*, and she did it, she wrapped a strip of bacon around the table leg and starts chewing, her lips glistening with grease, her whole face laughing, even her eyebrows and ears.

What face is she making right now? I hope, wherever she is, she's cracking up . . .

Inside floorboards creak as someone creeps toward the door. I wait for the *schwick tswh* of locks turning, the brassy rattling of the security chain swinging into the doorframe—Dante called those chains "hood wind chimes."

The footsteps stop.

"Terry, I hear you in there, man. I'm not leaving until you open up," I yell through the thick maroon door. I'm about to knock again when the door swings open.

Terry standing there, annoyed, like I'm trying to sell him something he doesn't want. "Bro, what?"

"You gotta tell Coach you changed your mind. That you want back on the team."

Terry laughs. "But I didn't and I don't. I don't even know why I tried out."

"Because you love ball, same as me. Same as D."

"Don't," Terry warns.

"I tried catching up with you at the town hall meeting."

Terry shrugs. "I saw you. I had to bounce. I had things to do."

"With your new friends, T? What kind of things are you—"

Terry cuts me off. "How's that your business?"

I throw my hands up in surrender. "Whoa," I say. "I'm asking because I'm worried."

"Why, Tone? Why you so worried about what I'm doing and who I'm doing it with? What, you made some kinda pledge to my dying brother to look after me or something? That it?"

"Terry, everyone knows those kids you're messing around with, they're trouble."

Anger flashes in Terry's eyes. "Maybe *I'm* trouble, too."

"Nah." I shake my head. "That's not you. The Terry I know is—"

"You don't know me, dude. Not anymore."

"Terry, I—"

"I'm only gonna tell you one time. *Fall back. Leave me alone.*"

"So all of a sudden you don't care about anything anymore?"

Terry takes a hard step toward me. "D cared. D cared a

lot. What'd that get him?" He jabs a finger into my chest. "You wanna turn my brother's death into some life lesson, but you don't even get it. The lesson is this: *You're either swinging or getting swung on.* And I'm done being a punching bag. I'm not dying on some jacked-up basketball court in the middle of the projects like my life ain't mean anything. Not me."

I swallow hard, wishing for the gazillionth time D was still here. D would know what to say. How to say it. But me? I'm all stutters—

"Terry, I—I—I just . . ."

"I told Coach to give you my spot on the team. So you wanna keep my brother alive dribbling a ball in some wack jersey, you go ahead. But me? I'm gonna make sure no one forgets D, my way."

"This isn't the answer, T. We're friends. We need to stick together."

Terry frowns. "Yeah, well, *friend,* you don't have the heart for this."

And then *kaaablaww*—a wind blast rushes against my face, the door slammed shut.

I don't go back to Big Mama's house. Not right away. I walk across the courtyard into the next tower over. Take the backstairs two by two until I'm on the third floor. I open our door, and I take a deep breath because even though it's only been a few days, I miss the smell of home.

On the bus ride to Big Mama's, my phone buzzes again. Another text, except this time it's from an unknown number.

**From Unknown**

Meet me at Bray tomorrow. I've got good news.

Because I guess this is how life comes at you—the good mixed with the bad.

# 2ND QUARTER

Coach is on a call when I knock.

"Well, how are these kids supposed to learn if they're freezing, John? This is America, *greatest nation in the world* everyone loves to say, but here we are with public schools without heat in one of the coldest regions of the country. Would you be okay if your kids sat in classrooms with icicles hanging from the ceiling?"

Coach waves me in, points to the chair opposite his desk. "Have a seat," he says.

*Have a seat* always makes me laugh. *Have a seat*, as if they're asking you take a chair home with you. Also, why is this chair so hard? Whoever made it obviously hates sitting.

Coach sets his phone down. "Sorry about that. How we doing?"

I shrug. "I could use some good news."

"I hear you." Coach folds his hands on his desk. "Listen, I know how much making this team meant to you. I'm sorry it didn't go the way you hoped."

I nod like it's all good. "I wasn't on my game at tryouts." I plaster on a smile. "Wasn't my day."

"No one busted their tail as hard as you, Tony. You should be proud of that. I'm proud of you."

I nod. "Thanks, Coach. Honestly, I wanted to hate, but there's no one on your roster that doesn't deserve their spot. Like you said, you gotta put the best team on the floor."

Coach shakes his head like he wishes it wasn't true. I study the photo on his desk. It's Coach on an NBA court, surrounded by four girls with bows and barrettes in their hair that match the jersey Coach is wearing. There's a woman, too. I'm guessing Coach's wife. All six of them smiling extra big. Like Big Mama says, *They're all teeth.*

"Tony, I want you on the team," Coach says, and I instantly snap outta my own head. "We could use your leadership. And your basketball IQ is off the charts. You play smart. You put the team first."

But all I hear is: *You on the team.*

Coach says *you on the team*, and my heart jetpacks through the ceiling I'm so happy.

Coach says *you on the team*, and now *I'm* all teeth, cheesing

90

so hard my cheeks might shatter.

But then Coach says, "But not as a player, Tony."

My stomach twists. My heart plummets. My brain scrambles. "Wait, what? How can I be on the team if I'm not playing?"

Coach opens his laptop and points the screen toward me. "Watch."

"Is this your highlight tape, Coach," I joke.

"Nah, we'd need a few weeks to watch my highlight reel, and we ain't got that kinda time." I laugh, and Coach grins. "No. This is last year's NBA playoffs."

"Oh, yeah, I remember this game. Gordon Quincy went off for fifty-six points." I remember that game well, GQ set a new franchise record for most points scored in a playoff elimination game.

"I want you to be our statistician," Coach says, pausing the video.

"Your statis-*what*?"

"Our statistician. You know those guys scribbling on clipboards and whispering stuff to the head coach or pointing out things to the players?"

"I guess," I say with a shrug. "But to be real, Coach, no one pays attention to those guys."

Coach nods. "Well, they're among the most valuable people on the whole team. And one of those guys is the statistician."

I appreciate Coach trying to include me on the team and

all, but I'm not buying this. He probably wants me to be the water boy or ball boy, and he's using this statistician stuff to disguise it. "What does he even do?"

"The statistician's job is to put everyone in the best possible position to win. Tone, you heard of analytics? Basically, you analyze each player's game, determine their strengths and weaknesses, and create a team game plan that best utilizes that information. Then you do the same thing for your opponents . . ."

I frown. "Wait, why would we help the other team?"

Coach laughs. "You're not. You're collecting their data. Looking for patterns in how they operate. Maybe you notice they always run a backdoor cut on a side-out-of-bounds play. You study their favorite lineups, where each player likes to shoot, or which hand they finish with in traffic. We learn their habits, strengths and weaknesses, and then we strategize our counterattack. You follow?"

"I think so," I say. Except I want to tell Coach, *I appreciate you looking out for me, but you're wasting your time. I can't do it. I wanna be on the court, in the game, and you're handing me a clipboard, like I'm forty-five years old. I don't wanna coach. I wanna play.* "Look, Coach, I'mma be real, this ain't for me. What do I know about strategy? About analyzing patterns?"

"You're a point guard, right? You already do this. You notice mismatches. You look for holes in the other team's game that the team can exploit. Right?"

"The thing is, it would be torture to be with the team but never play. To never put on our team jersey. To never hear my number called."

Coach nods. "I'm calling your number right now. So, you coming into the game or not?"

# 14

I'm ducking outta Bray when Munka hits me.

**From Munka**

So when we celebrating!?!

I wait until I'm on the bus to Big Mama's to text back:

Um celebrating what??

She replies instantly—I swear sometimes it's like she's already responding to texts I haven't even sent yet.

Her reply is zero percent shocking since I'm pretty sure Munka believes the only reason she even has eyes are to roll them in disgust at whoever's annoying her.

Followed by a spinning basketball gif because this is what Munka does—always too much.

Okay, somehow Munka knows about my meeting with Coach James.

And she's assuming, the way I did, that Coach wanted to put me on the team.

But how does Munka know?

Before I can even think about it, my phone's buzzing like mad.

You've been tagged by AyoKO.

I tap the IG notification and a video of my head—only three times bigger—pasted on a janitor's body, and Janitor Tony's plunging a disgusting toilet with brown water splashing everywhere. I read the caption:

Tony will do anything to make the team hahaha

#dedication #gross

The video's only been posted seventeen minutes, but it's already got 102 likes and 24 comments, a few from guys on the team.

@ZayAllDay24: Not cool, KO.

@SpecialKBeastMode13: WOW, you crazy dude 😂 😂 😂

But I don't read any more. I want to hit back at KO. Embarrass *him*, like, *Bro, isn't your dad a janitor?* My phone buzzes with more notifications, and for a second, I fantasize about throwing my phone out the bus window, watching it smack the sidewalk, shattering just like my dreams of making the Sabres, of doing D proud.

Only, none of that will make me feel better.

None of that will change anything.

Because facts—I *don't* have what it takes.

D did.

KO does.

But not me.

# 15

This statistician job?

Maybe I don't know a lot about AAU ball, but I've never heard of somebody sitting there scribbling numbers in some notebook while everyone else was, you know, playing the game?

For real, it feels like Coach pulled this statistician job outta his butt. Like, *Let's toss Tone a bone, make him feel better.*

Everyone else is smashing whole T-bone steaks, but me? I'm gnawing on a bone no one wants.

I'm *tired* of chewing old bones. I'm tired of people throwing me scraps *they* don't even want.

I'm tired of people behind desks telling me how awful they feel for me.

I'm tired of people promising, *If you work hard, you can do anything. You can achieve your dreams.*

Coach said it himself—I bust my butt every day. Every week, I get up two thousand jumpers. Five days a week, I run five miles. I say, *Nah, I'm good* to my favorite candy. I turn down my favorite snacks. Yo, I pass on Big Mama's cobbler.

All that for what?

So I can *analyze numbers and patterns* like the nerdiest human calculator of all time?

I know who I am. I keep it real with myself because who else will?

So, no, I'm never gonna have the freshest gear. And I probably won't grow another inch. What you see? It's what you get.

But I promise you:

I always give my everything.

And for what? To end up in the same spot I started? A player without a team. Without a coach teaching me to win. Without people believing I could matter.

I don't want your handouts. I don't need or want your sorrys. What little I got, I love cuz I earned it. Every bit. But most of all? I want *you* to know I belong here. That I'm just as good as you.

And okay, maybe I wanna know I belong, too. Maybe I need to know I'm good enough.

What I do know is no matter the score, or the matchup, I fight until the clock strikes zero. I hold nothing back. I leave everything on the floor. Because if there's anything D's death taught me?

You better play every game like it's your very last.

"I know this isn't what you wanna hear, but you should consider Coach's offer," Big Mama says, handing me an extra-large bowl of cobbler, because why keep denying myself the things I love if I'm never gonna see the court?

I shrug. "That really what you think, or is this a *grown-up teaching you a life lesson* moment?"

Big Mama laughs and throws a dish towel at me. "Boy, if you aren't just like your daddy . . ."

I frown. "He wishes."

Big Mama sits down beside me and dips a spoon deep into my bowl, scooping a chunk of juicy peach before I can stop her. Not that I would've tried—it's just the principle. "He wishes what?"

"Dad wishes he had a son that was more like him. That was better at ball. Taller. Stronger. Just better."

Big Mama wags her head. "You sure that's not what *you* wish?"

"Big Mama, when's the last time you been in Dad's old room? There's like a hundred trophies with his name on them. For real, the other night I woke up and I was cuddling one like a body pillow!"

Big Mama cracks up. "Yep, so silly, just like your daddy."

I tap my spoon against the side of my bowl. "Feels like most days we couldn't be any more different."

Big Mama shakes her head. "He said the same thing, you know? Your father. He didn't think he measured up to his dad, either."

My face scrunches. "Wait, Granddad Arthur? He was disappointed in Dad?"

"Not even a little bit. He was proud of your dad, the same way your dad's proud of you. But that didn't stop your dad from sitting in the same chair you sitting in with those same sad puppy-dog eyes, asking me, *How come Papa don't love me like he loves my sisters?*"

"What'd you tell him?"

Big Mama reaches for another spoonful of cobbler, and I push the bowl closer to her.

"I told him what I'm telling you. That your dad loves you more than he loves himself. That he loves you so hard and so much he doesn't have the words to tell you."

"And what did Dad say then?"

"Same thing you're wondering."

I smile. "Oh, you a mind reader now?"

Big Mama winks. "No, not now. I've always been."

Now it's my turn to laugh. "Big Mama, you're so silly," I tease. "But okay, what did Dad say after you told him that?"

Big Mama leans back in her chair. "With his voice cracking on every syllable, he said, *But, Mama, it only takes three words, and you say them all the time. Why can't Papa?"*

"Wait, you mean Dad started crying?"

Big Mama's face sharpens. "What? You don't think your dad's human? You don't think he got feelings, same as you, that get hurt?"

"I just can't see Dad crying."

"Listen to me, Tony. Strong men? They cry. They cry good. Because crying isn't weak. Crying means you care."

"Dad says I'm too sensitive."

"He shouldn't. You're not," Big Mama says, sucking her teeth. "No one's got any business telling someone else how they should feel. Even parents get it wrong sometimes."

"Ha, have you met my father? He's never wrong."

Big Mama turns her head toward the kitchen window. Stares out at the backyard. At the greenest grass in the neighborhood. At the patch of sunflowers standing tall against the breeze. At the baby-blue birdhouse hanging from a tree, swaying in the wind. At the small brown bird swooping through the branches.

Until finally, Big Mama, eyes still on the window, says, "Your granddad wanted what every parent wants for their kids."

The bird flies round and round the birdhouse, like it's not sure if it's safe. "What's that?"

"Bigger and better," Big Mama says. "We want our kids to have everything we couldn't. We want them to have more. Tony . . ." Big Mama pauses, as if she's turning over each word in her head like a stone before handing them to me. "Your dad. He's trying. He's messing up, too. Same as his dad. Same as me. Same as you. But he's trying, and for every time he gets it wrong, there are three or four where he almost gets it just right. That's not an excuse. I'm going to talk to him about calling you sensitive."

"No!" I sit up quick. "I don't want him to know I said anything."

Big Mama smiles. "He won't. All these years and your daddy still can't read me." She takes one last bite of cobbler. "Besides, I told your granddad the same thing."

My eyebrows lift. "That he shouldn't call Dad sensitive?"

Big Mama wipes a bit of cobbler from her lip. "And that he should tell your dad he loved him more, yes."

"And did he?" I ask.

Big Mama makes a face—but not being able to read her must be hereditary, because I have no clue what she's thinking.

"He tried," she says softly, like she's still deciding.

And Big Mama and I watch the brown bird land on the birdhouse. We watch it poke its black beak into the mountain of seeds, its eyes widening and its wings fluttering like it's hit the jackpot, snapping the shells in half and munching, munching.

# 16

Big Mama's right.

It *is* worth thinking about.

So I think and I decide.

**To Coach James**

Thanks for the offer, Coach but I'm gonna pass.
Good luck this season!

I tap send, and I imagine those two sentences zipping through the air, flying through walls, like two photon torpedoes, before buzzing in their target's shorts pocket. I try to picture his face as he reads it. But all I see is D, spinning a basketball, his dark eyes staring at me like, *What are you doing, Tone?*

Even though I know he's not really there, I answer anyway. "You don't get it. D, Coach *knew* I wasn't gonna take that job. He offered because he feels sorry for me."

D spins the ball faster, his eyes still locked on mine.

I shrug. I feel my blood warming, my heart speeding up. "Would you have taken it? Huh? Of course not, because you would've made the team. It's easy when you're naturally great at everything you do, right? But see, I wouldn't know that, D. That was you not me. I'm not a winner like you. And I'm never gonna be, okay? So don't you stand there, judging me. This is *my* life. I gotta live it the way I want, just like you lived . . . just like you lived . . ."

My throat burns. "Why'd you leave me, man? You're supposed to be here. How come it was you, man? How come it wasn't me? Why am I still here and you're gone forever? I don't have anything to offer anybody. I can't ball. I can't draw. I can't rap. I can't do nothing. What's my talent? What's my strength? I work hard. That's what everybody says, right? But where did that get me? Where did that get you? Man, why'd you have to go? Huh? Answer me, dude, why'd you leave me?"

But D doesn't argue with me. He doesn't say a word. He shakes his head, tosses me the ball, and walks away.

# 17

My pillow's glued to the side of my face when the buzzing wakes me up. I figure it's a reply from Coach, but nope, it's our family group text.

**From Mom**

I love you. I miss you.

I rub my eyes, then open them wide to make sure I'm seeing right.

How many times had me and Mom split couch cushions where she'd reach over and touch my ear or the back of my head, studying me like she's making sure I'm real, and I'd snap, *Mom, stop being weird.*

Ha, what I wouldn't give now to see her hand reaching

for me, her fingers massaging my head, squeezing my neck.
*I love you*, she always said. But I didn't always say it back.
Too many times I hit her with *I know, Mom*, my eyes already
refocusing on the TV or my phone.

But if she was here, sitting on the edge of my bed, I'd
say it right back. Over and over again, a hundred times, a
thousand times. However many times she needed to know
I meant it.

But she's not here.

**To Mom**

I love you MORE

A thing I'd sometimes say to her, a game we played where
she'd laugh and say, *Impossible, kid. Impossible.*

I'm brushing my teeth when my phone starts dancing on
the sink.

**From Coach James**

Yoo, Tony, don't ever come to the gym again!!

😂 😂 😂

I'm just messing with you. That's probably a bad
joke. My kids say I'm even cornier than normal
first thing in the morning, especially before I had
my coffee, so it's not my fault! Lol

Anyway, I obviously got your text and I'm not
gonna lie, Tone. I'm disappointed. We could use
that brain of yours!! And trust me, I get how it's
not the way you imagined, Tony.

But you've always struck me as a kid who only
cared about what was best for the team. You

could help this team win, on and off the court. But I understand how you feel. I know it's hard when your heart's set on one thing, and you don't get it.

But a word of advice? Don't let pride keep you from walking in through a door just because it's not the front door. In the end, it still gets you inside the house.

And yeah, you better be at the games cheering so loud people think you're the mascot, you hear me?? Hahaha. Anyway, if you need anything, or if you change your mind, you can always reach out, day or night. Stay up!

I read Coach's texts a few times before I begin typing a reply.

I got you, mascot mentality on lock!!

But I delete it because that's not how I really feel.

Because it's easier to make stupid jokes than to admit my brain feels like it's on fire.

Because if you're laughing at my stupid jokes, then maybe you won't see that heart's like a puzzle with pieces lost forever.

Because it's easier to spit out a stupid joke than telling you, *I'm the kind of sad you maybe never get over.*

*I'm the kind of sad you live with, like a scar. One day you'll forget how you looked without it.*

I delete it because what if I'm making a mistake?

# 18

Dad gets a text message saying there's gonna be a protest, followed by a candlelight vigil, at OS—the hope was if the community rallied together, showed solidarity, and let everyone know they weren't about to drop the cause anytime soon, it might force the mayor or the district attorney to reopen the investigation into D's death.

"We're going, right?" I ask Dad as he packs up leftovers to take to work.

Dad zips his lunch bag closed and stares at me, like *What you think?* "How could we *not* go? Dante was family when he was alive, and he's still family now."

Big Mama buys a bunch of candles and other supplies

and—together with me and Tasha—drops them off at the community center, where maybe a couple dozen volunteers wearing *#REMEMBERDANTE* shirts move about accepting donations and organizing the inventory.

"You really think a bunch of people holding candles in the dark is gonna make a difference?" I ask Big Mama, not because I'm being a smart mouth but because I really wanna know.

Like, how will a protest and vigil change anything when other protests and community meetings haven't done squat?

Big Mama nods. "Anything we can do to draw attention to injustice, we gotta try it. We gotta let the powers that be know it's not over. We're not going anywhere until justice prevails."

"We appreciate this," a Black woman wearing a red head-wrap says, accepting the bags the three of us are carrying.

"We've all gotta chip in," Big Mama says. "Every bit helps."

Big Mama's talking to a few older people from OS while Tasha loads candles into boxes with one of the volunteers—and I don't know, seeing all of this makes my heart happy, makes me proud that no one's ready to move on. That everyone's working together even though it feels like the people in power just want it to be over already.

I slip outside for air, turning the corner for the parking lot, when I spot the last person I expected to see. Terry's posted up against the side of the same SUV as before—with its tinted windows, black rims, and those bright purple lights—it's hard to forget.

"Sup," I say, scanning the parking lot for his new friends.

"Sup," Terry repeats. For a moment, it feels like we're both about to talk at the same time but it passes like a cloud, and neither of us says a word. Terry checks his phone and I move gravel around with my shoe.

"Sorry about the decision . . ." I say finally. "But I'm glad you're here. Every bit helps," I say, stealing Big Mama's line.

"I ran into Coach," Terry says, ignoring my words. "Said he was holding a spot open for me. I told him that was supposed to be my gift to you."

I nod slowly. "Thanks, anyway, but I don't wanna make the team like that."

Terry grins, but it's not a happy smile. "It's not fair, you know?"

"What's not fair?"

"This. Any of it. My brother works hard, still ends up taking a dirt nap. You work hard, they tell you you're not good enough. Me? I don't want the team, and here's Coach like *The door's always open*. World don't make sense."

"Maybe not," I agree. "So, be real, you think this vigil will make a difference?"

"The truth?" Terry's face hardens. "If we want any real change around here, we're gonna have to make it happen ourselves, feel me?"

I shake my head. "What's that supposed to mean?"

Terry shrugs. "It means sooner or later, we're gonna catch up to Officer Truman and make sure he gets his."

And on cue, the SUV windows roll down, all of Terry's new friends staring at me, their eyes dark, their faces as sharp as knives—and there, in the front seat, sits the king of them all, Khalil.

"Tony-Tone. Ain't see you in a minute," Khalil says. "Figured you left for Harvard or got a job at Google." Everyone in the SUV cracks up.

The way D dominated the courts, Khalil dominates the streets. D and Khalil grew up together—they were tight, too—but while D stayed focused on ball, Khalil stayed in trouble, and eventually, even though he didn't want to, D cut ties with Khalil.

"Terry, this stuff with D? With Truman? It's not right. No one's arguing about that. But you can't just make your own justice."

"Truman did," Terry says. "And you know I can't just let that slide. So, now *he's* on the clock."

"Tonyyyyyyyyy," Tasha scream-sings my name behind me. I turn around, and she's running hard straight for me in a *#JUSTICEFORDANTE* T-shirt a couple sizes too big, a wide grin on her face. I return her smile and pivot back to Terry and his friends.

But Terry's climbing into the back seat of the SUV. "You got your hands full, bro," he says.

"Tonyyyyyyyy, come oooooonnn, alreadyyyyyyy!"

I motion for Tasha to quiet down. "Sorry, my bad. Hey, maybe if you're gon—"

Before I can ask if he's going to the Sabres' first game tomorrow, Terry waves me off. "Nah, chill, bro. Go enjoy your family. We don't know how much time we got with them, you know?"

## MILWAUKEE, WISCONSIN

The guys are warming up.

A few are taking shots and chasing rebounds. Zay's got a ball in each hand, dribbling down the sideline. And Special K's crouching up and down, a rubber resistance band tethering his legs, with Coach James telling him when to pause and restart. Special K hardly played last year—our middle school coach said he was too weak in the paint. And I like Special K, but Coach was right. He got pushed around like he was a swinging door. Except Special K's insisting this year is gonna be different. *I've been working out, eating right*, he kept saying at tryouts, every time someone said something about his new physique. I don't know a lot about weight lifting, but I do know Special K got ripped over this last year. Dude looks like if he breathes too hard his jersey might rip right down the middle like he's Clark Kent changing clothes. *Yo, I'm in the best shape I've been in since I came out my moms.*

Meanwhile, the starters—ha, they're all posted up at half-court, stretching and cheesing, pointing at the bleachers and laughing. As always, KO's literally at center court holding court, balancing on one foot while he holds his other foot against his butt, stretching his quad.

I don't even gotta hear their conversation to know KO's probably swearing some girl's in love with him. Only thing KO loves talking about more than how many triple-doubles he's gonna put up are girls.

I slide over to make room for Big Mama. She shakes her head at me. "Don't even ask me where I had to park."

I smile. "That bad?"

"Let's just say, I got all my steps in for the month."

The Sabres win the jump ball—which is cool.

Coach is all about *starting fast* and *dominating early*.

Except that jump ball? Yeah, it's the first and last thing the Sabres win for the *rest of the first half.*

The Hoosiers take care of the ball. At halftime, they only have three turnovers. But the Sabres? They have four turnovers in their first six possessions, and nine for the half.

They're outrebounded 19–10.

Combined, the team only has five assists, and all five came from two players: Meeks (3) and Zay (2).

In other words, it's sixteen minutes of super-ugly basketball. Even Big Mama's frustrated and she barely cares about ball. "Make it stop. Please, make it stop," she keeps muttering to herself.

The Titusville Tigers pounce their way to a 21–7 lead.

As hard to watch as this game is, it's harder to watch Coach. The whole first half, he stalks the sideline calling plays, shouting encouragement, and yelling for everyone to:

*C'mon, push it!*

*Dig deep!*

*Play with heart! Show me some heart!*

Honestly, I feel bad for Coach even more than the guys—because at least Coach isn't giving up. Not even when the Tigers' lead balloons to nineteen points. Because blowouts aren't on the coaches. Blowouts happen for one of two reasons—

1. *Not enough talent.* Except I've done my homework—Titusville is basically running the same squad they had last year, minus their second-best player, who jumped ship for another South Cali team. Meanwhile, our Sabres have two players ranked in the top fifty eighteen-and-under players in the entire country—KO and Meeks; and KO's in the top fifteen.

So, talent isn't it.

Why Blowouts Happen Reason #2:

2. *Attitude.* The team doesn't play for each other. Everyone cares more about self than team. They quit on each other.

And while I don't think the team's quit on Coach *yet*, anyone with half a basketball brain can see they're not trusting each other. No one has anyone's back out there on the court.

Which means, from the very start, even before the ref tossed the jump ball into the air, before the time official started the game clock, the Sabres were DOA.

Defeated On Arrival.

Even with better play in the second half, the hole's too big to climb out of—and the Hoosiers blow out the Sabres by sixteen. And honestly, it wasn't even *that* close.


I barely get half a Converse in the locker room when— *bzzzzp*—I'm zapped, my whole body lit up brighter than an X-mas tree in an X-ray machine, a victim of the force field known as the Sad Boy Super Shield.

Yep, that's right, a *bad vibes only, we feel sorry for ourselves* force field.

I was gonna stroll in dishing out compliments like assists, like *Hey, DJ, way to rotate out there! Special K, that putback you had in the third? My face hurts just from watching, it was so savage! Zay and J-Wu, y'all locked your men up that second half*—because of course the guys would be down after a loss. But this?

This is *sad boy energy* on ten.

It's scary quiet, too. Normally, there's music blasting, players dancing and hollering as they search the game hashtag for their highlights and make plans to grab burritos at Don Tequila's, dudes crashing into lockers, reenacting that killer crossover that broke so-and-so's ankles—*ohmigod, you broke him off, son.*

This atmosphere, yeah, this ain't it.

This is the realization that maybe you aren't as good as you thought.

This is realizing that not only are you not good enough to win it all in Orlando, you're not even good enough to be *invited* to the tournament.

"Yo, way to grab those boards, Special K," I say as I pass by. He barely nods.

I bump fists with Zay. "Bro," he says, wagging his head. "We just got run over by a Mack Truck, for real."

I shrug, looking for something positive to say. "It's only the first game. You guys will get better, watch."

I find Coach in the back of the locker room, just as he drops his whistle into his bag.

Seriously, I get using it at practice, but I don't get why he wears it during games, sometimes even letting it hang from his lips like he's a backup ref—like he's gonna coach *and* officiate the game.

Can you imagine those game stats?

REPORTER: *Coach-Ref James, you only called one foul on*

*the Sabres the entire game. But you called 187 fouls on the visiting team. Care to address the discrepancy?*

*COACH-REF JAMES: Yeah, that foul I called on the Sabres was an inadvertent whistle, to be honest. I would've called zero fouls. What can I say about that team except they are incredibly well coached!*

"Hey, good game, Coach," I say out of habit. *Good game,* a thing you say to the other team whether you win or lose. But Coach frowns, and I immediately regret it.

Coach shakes his head. "Were we watching the same game? We got drubbed out there."

I make a mental note to look up *drubbed* later, but I'd bet money it means *we got our butts whupped bad.*

I slide my hands into my pockets to make myself smaller. I imagine myself shrinking to the size of a peanut. Basically, I'd be invisible; which would be cool because then I wouldn't be the dude who just complimented a Milwaukee hoops legend on a game where his team lost by fifteen points. Wait, my bad—sixteen points.

But my brain votes *not* to miniaturize me, *and* then has the nerve to say something super unauthorized:

"Hey, Coach? You still looking for a statistician?"

# 20

I hop off the bus, my backpack shouldered, my ball under my other arm, thinking, *Tony, be conscientious.*

Which is a four-syllable word for: *work hard, pay attention, be dependable.*

That's our deal—Coach said, *You wanna be a part of this team, you gotta be conscientious. If not, you should skip it. You wanna sit on that sideline, you work hard every day—especially the days you don't feel like it. This is bigger than you. Bigger than me. We win together; we lose together. Being conscientious means constantly asking yourself:*

*What am I doing to help this team? Notice I didn't say to help this team win. I said, help, period. Because what you and I do is never about the scoreboard; it's always about the people. One huddle, one hustle, one head, one heart.*

*Be at tomorrow's practice*, Coach says.

I figure I'm here to watch the guys run drills, maybe take notes.

But I barely say what's up to the guys before Coach steers me into his office. He tosses me a TV remote and a laptop.

"The game film's on the laptop. It'll beam onto the TV," Coach says, rushing out the door.

"Wait, where are you going?"

Coach laughs, pokes his head back inside. "I have a practice to run."

I scrunch my face. "Okay, but what am I supposed to be doing?"

"You remember watching film with D, yeah? This is just like that. You study our opponents. Look for patterns. Take notes. Report back to me."

I nod. *Observe, record, report.*

Seems simple enough.

Not even thirty minutes later, I'm scribbling *the Wolves play man-to-man defense 80% of the time* when she walks in. I don't pause the game tape because I figure it's Coach checking on me or grabbing something from his office.

But then she says, "Tony, right?" I nod as she snatches keys from Coach's desk. "I'm Kiara. Sorry, just grabbing these and I'll be outta your way."

Except before I can say *It's cool*, she's gone. I guess quick exits run in the family.

Well, almost.

She spins around on her sneaker heels, her eyes fixed on the TV. "Wow, they really sell out on their full-court press, huh? Well, nothing a strong crosscourt pass can't beat, right?" Folding her arms, she walks closer to the mounted TV.

And in less time than an NBA shot clock, I already know three things to be absolutely, undeniably true about Kiara James:

1. She's crazy beautiful.
2. She knows as much, if not more, about basketball than me.
3. When I look at her, I'm gonna feel things. Lots of things.

And you're thinking—*Wow, Tone, how you rev from zero to a hundred so quick?*

Honestly, all I can tell you is:

She's got that kind of voice that makes you wanna lose a whole night on the phone even though you *hate* phone calls so much, your favorite basketball player could call you right now and you'd be like, *Ugh, what you want?*

She's got the kind of voice that makes you happy just hearing it. It's tough and confident and a little bit raspy, which I didn't even know I liked until literally just now when I heard her talk.

Another thing—she makes me . . . I don't know . . . I

guess, nervous? Not because she's a girl. Most of my family are girls. So *why* I feel that way right now, I can't even call it.

I almost forget she's still there until she laughs, her eyes locked on mine. "Tony, you okay?"

"Huh?" I hear myself say back. "Who? Me?"

*Dude, duh, you, you're the only other person in the room, get your head in the game.*

She laughs again. "Yeah, you. Unless there's someone hiding in the room I don't see." I can tell she's smiling, even though I've turned back to the TV.

Which, she probably thinks I'm rude or annoyed she's here, but really, I'm just trying to not melt into Tony mush.

"You don't talk much, huh?" she asks.

*C'mon, Tony, look up, look up. You're being stupid and you don't even know why, so just stop*, I tell myself.

"Well, I didn't mean to bother you," she says, her voice changing so that it sounds sad but also maybe like she's gonna leave, neither of which I want. I force my eyes to look at her.

"Oh, hey, hi, hello there," I stammer. Why my brain spits out three different greetings in two seconds, I can't explain it.

She smiles. "Okay, well, I'm pretty good with finding patterns and devising strategies, so," she says, without blinking. Which makes me notice how often *I'm* blinking. Which the answer is *too much*. "If you ever want some help . . ."

Her voice trails off, leaving space for me to answer.

"Yes! Help! Cool!" I spit out using fewer words than I

wanted while using more enthusiasm than any three words have ever needed.

This cracks her up, though—and yeah, she could just be laughing at me, but honestly, surprisingly that doesn't bother me.

She can totally laugh at me.

"Dad said you were smart, but he didn't say you were funny, too."

"It's usually not on purpose," I admit. This time we both laugh.

"So, listen, if we're gonna work together, we gotta get one thing clear. Yes, I'm the coach's daughter, but I run on my own two feet. So, don't treat me any differently. I hate when people do that. Cool?"

"Yeah, I got you."

"You gotta promise."

"What am I promising?"

"Promise me that you'll judge me, Kiara Marie James, only based on *me*, Kiara Marie James."

"I promise."

"Good. I promise you, too." She slides into Coach's desk chair. "Should we get started, then?"

I motion toward the keys in her hand. "Don't you gotta get those to Coach?"

She laughs. "No, the keys were an excuse to talk to you. I don't even know what they open."

Two hours fly by like the speed of light, and I don't know what's more surprising—how fast time is moving, or how many pages of notes Kiara and I have between us, watching and rewinding the Wolves film from their last three games.

I'm tapping open the last game when the office door sails open.

Kiara's face turns worried. "Dad, is everything okay?"

"Huh?" Coach says, his face hard to read. "Oh, uh, yeah, everything's . . . I just wanted to check on you two, see how it's going in here."

I nod. "It's going great, Coach. Better than I expected, to be honest."

Coach's eyebrows slide upward, his voice deepening. "How's that?"

I glance over at Kiara, then back to Coach. "Kiara knows *so* much about basketball. I can't even tell you how much stuff she's taught me already."

Kiara grins. "Learned from the best," she says, winking at Coach.

"Ha, yeah, well, if you guys need anything, I'll probably run the guys another hour or so . . ."

"Cool, we're good, Dad."

"You know, Tone, the only thing I love more than basketball is my family."

"Sure, Coach. Makes sense."

But Coach isn't finished. "And my daughters are my

whole world. Feel me?"

Except the way Coach asks the question, it's clear there's only one right answer: "Yes, sir. I do."

"Good." Coach rubs his forehead. "Good," he says again. "Glad we had that talk."

Kiara shakes her head. "Okay, we got it, you came in, you flexed your muscles, great. But Tony and I have a lot of work to do."

"Right. I should let you get back to it, I guess," Coach says.

"Hey, Coach, did Terry show up?"

Coach shakes his head. "Afraid not."

I nod, try to make my face smile.

"He's a smart kid," Coach says. "He's gonna figure it out."

"I hope so," I say back.

Coach nods, before slipping outta his office with way more chill than how he came.

# 21

Except Terry's doing the opposite of figuring it out.

*"We have breaking news. Three suspects were taken into police custody for allegedly harassing local law enforcement agent Officer Samuel Eli Truman. Earlier this month, Officer Truman was involved in the controversial shooting death of national hoops phenom Dante Jones, an incident that city officials are now calling a sad but completely by-the-book encounter.*

*According to reports, fourteen-year-old Terry Jones, the younger brother of Dante Jones, is among the three suspects.*

*Allegedly, the three young men followed Officer Truman*

*after he concluded his shift at the Thirty-Fourth Precinct, to his home in Pewaukee, eventually making threats that left Officer Truman fearful for his life.*

*Authorities have said it is still too early to determine whether Dante's tragic death played a role in the actions of the three suspects, all of whom are minors, under the age of seventeen.*

*The suspects are expected to be charged as early as this evening . . ."*

Even though I know he probably doesn't have his phone, I still text him, anyway.

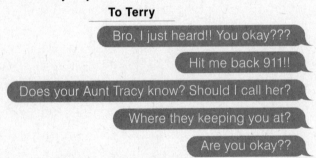

**To Terry**

> Bro, I just heard!! You okay???

> Hit me back 911!!

> Does your Aunt Tracy know? Should I call her?

> Where they keeping you at?

> Are you okay??

I beg Dad and Big Mama to let me visit him—to take me to wherever it is they're holding Terry. Dad talks to Aunt Tracy—the only family Terry's got now that D's gone—and she says Terry's okay but he's not allowed visitors yet.

"But they're gonna let him call me this afternoon, so if there's anything you want me to tell him, I'll pass it on."

I nod and try to think of something important to say, something that'll maybe convince Terry that there's a better way to use his pain. That as bad as we all wanna see Officer Truman pay, Terry's only hurting himself. He's being the "monster" they already believe we are.

"Tell him I still believe in him," I finally say to Aunt Tracy.

# 22

No matter what, I can't stop worrying about Terry—is he okay, is he afraid, are they ever gonna let him out? So I do what I always do when I'm distracting my brain from whatever it's obsessed with, like when Mom's having an Other Day and there's nothing I can do to make it Good—I pick up a ball and start shooting.

Well, technically, I watch other people shoot, because I spend the next several practices fully buried in game film. I watch our team's game film and Kiara's recorded practices. I even ask Coach to get the game film from each player's junior high squad, and I analyze that, too. In one week, I've reviewed twenty-three games' worth of film, and I have a notebook filled with numbers, stats, and notes to prove it.

It's wild—I can't lie, at first, I kept wishing I was on the court with the guys, but the more film I studied, the more patterns and plays I understood, the more I like this statistician thing.

You can learn so much about a team, about every player and coach, just by watching and paying attention. They say the ball don't lie—well, the numbers don't, either. You just gotta know how to get the full story.

Like, our team's field goal percentage in the paint is an impressive 63 percent.

But our three-point percentage is 31 percent.

Which seems kinda bad, except when you realize that Special K's and DJ's individual three-ball percentage is 21 and 24 and that they've taken 21 percent of the team's overall threes.

You subtract their awful shooting, and our team percentage jumps to 39 percent, which is among the best in the country in our age group.

See, what I mean—it's not enough to say we don't shoot the three ball well, because that's not the whole truth. I tell Coach and he's like, *This is what I'm talking about. This is the kind of numbers I can show these guys so they know I'm not just giving them a hard time. Now there's evidence to back me up. This is really good stuff, Tony.*

And I feel good. Great even.

Except all those stats got me wondering if that's how things work in real life, too.

Like, on the surface, you might decide exactly how you feel about a person. You might feel like you know their whole story, that you know everything worth knowing. Plus, you've got the stats, facts, and receipts to prove it.

But here's the thing, we can work the math to support what we wanna believe . . . or we can dig a bit deeper, open our heart a little wider, and let the numbers speak for themselves.

Let them give you the whole story.

Coach blows the whistle, and the team gathers around him, same as any other practice.

Coach usually finishes with a few words of encouragement, while challenging the team to work harder, to keep pushing to get better.

"Two things we need to talk about," Coach says. "One, we all know what happened with Terry, that he's in juvie. And while we don't ever condone violence or taking the law into our own hands, there is good news to be shared. Because of all the national attention Terry's arrest has caused, the local police are getting hundreds of phone calls and letters from all over the country, with people insisting they let Terry go and that the prosecutor take a harder look at bringing Officer Truman to justice. Also, there's gonna be a protest and candlelight vigil held in Dante's honor in a few days, and I hope we'll all be there. If you need a ride, just let me know."

And it's weird, how you can feel everyone, including

Coach, take a deep breath. Like, obviously this is good news. News that we're happy to hear. But also, the news we wanna hear most is: Terry's free and Dante's killer is behind bars.

Coach clears his throat, and I figure the second thing we need to talk about is really just gonna be Coach giving us those post-practice encouraging words.

So, I'm caught off guard when instead he nods at me and says: "A lot of you are wondering why Tony's been here . . ."

C'mon, Coach, don't do this. Not now. I'm not in the mood for jokes. KO's face is already lighting up with something smart to say, I can tell.

"Tony is joining our squad as statistician."

"Dang, he even found a way to nerd up the basketball team," KO says, right on cue. Half the team cracks up.

But Coach shoots them a look, and they stop instantly.

"Which means that sometimes he'll practice with us and work out with us," Coach continues. "But mostly, he'll analyze, scout, and prep us for games. He has my full support, and I expect you to treat him as a teammate. Questions?"

"Yeah," Special K says, raising his hand. "What's a statistician? Ooh, they the dudes that be pulling rabbits outta hats, right?"

**23**

Last week, we were ranked number eleven in the country in the preseason polls. But after our Hoosiers loss, the Hoosiers jump from number fifteen to number eleven while we plummet to number twenty-two. Which, when your goal's to be the last team standing in Orlando, kinda sucks.

"That's flagrantly disrespectful, wow," Meeks says, shaking his head. "How they do us like that? Bro, we dropped faster than Tower of Terror."

"How you know that? Your butt ain't been to Disneyland," DJ says, laughing.

And we all crack up, Meeks, too. "First of all, it's Disney *World*, not Land. Get it right."

"But seriously, we lose one game and they act like the sky's falling," KO complains. "It's stupid."

"Dumb stupid," Special K agrees, shaking his fists in the air like he's gonna fight every team ranked ahead of us.

But Coach isn't nearly as emotional. "Nothing's given to us," he says, lifting his whistle to begin our last practice before our next tournament. "We get what we earn."

Boarding the team bus, I'm thinking one thing.

Okay, *two* things.

Thing 2: *Don't trip and fall in the aisle.* The embarrassment is real.

Thing 1: *D should be here.*

D should be standing next to me in this Bray parking lot, his drawstring backpack drooping from his shoulders protecting his brand-new sneakers inside, in one hand a gallon jug of spring water—he drank water like it actually tastes good, which, ugh—and in his other hand his long fingers clutching a rolled-up, greasy brown paper bag, because here's a secret about D—

My man *loved* fast-food breakfast.

The way some people love cars, or their pets, or themselves—yeah, D loved fast-food breakfast menus.

His go-to order: *two breakfast burritos with extra picante and a large OJ.*

Oh, and every week, he asked the same question: *What kind of pies y'all got in there?*

The two of us should be yawning and stretching and, I don't know, talking about what we ate for dinner, while we wait to board this bus—nicest bus I've ever seen—at the god-ugly hour of five o'clock in the morning. I should be laughing as he hits me with the latest call or text from college recruiters, all those big-time schools still begging him to take their scholarship—all, *D, c'mon, man, tell me what it's gonna take to get you here, you name it and it's yours*, even though he announced Duke as his choice weeks ago.

And okay, yes, D was on the high school varsity team, he was two or three years older than all of us, so no, he wouldn't have boarded this bus as our teammate, but . . . I still imagine him here, even if to wave us off. Cuffing his hands together like a megaphone and shouting after us, as our long bus trudged down the road, *Y'all got this. I'mma see you there!*

Plus, I know *if D was here, Terry would be, too.*

But they're not.

And no matter how many times I look, they're never gonna be here.

When I finally step up onto the bus, I pause at the top of the stairs, looking at everyone and everything.

"What, you got a flare for the dramatic, son?" the bus driver asks me.

"What do you mean?"

"I mean, we ain't all extras in the story of *your* life, so hurry up and sit your slow butt down, we got places to go, tournaments to win."

I smile and slide into the first empty seat, across from Coach; Kiara waves from the window seat next to him. I wave back, and Coach asks, "You ready?"

I nod. "I was born ready," I say, not smiling.

But Kiara bursts out laughing. "Ugh, it's too early for y'all to be so corny."

Coach grins. "Why you ruining our moment?"

But she's busy popping in earbuds, still laughing to herself.

"Born ready," Coach repeats. "I like it."

And yeah, it *is* corny.

But it's better than my real answer:

*I'm just trying not to throw up.*


Keep it all the way real, I kinda hoped Kiara and I would sit together on the bus so we could, you know, review the stats we've analyzed and double-check our strategy. Even if she just switched spots with Coach, that would be cool, too— then we'd only have the aisle separating us. An hour into the trip, Coach slides out to let Kiara use the bus bathroom, and I smile, thinking maybe she'll come back and make Coach scoot over to the window.

But Coach stands up and she's back at the window. She's about to put her earbuds in when she leans forward and shakes her head.

"You're not tired?" she asks.

I shrug. "I haven't been sleeping that great."

"Well, please, try now," she says. "I'm not trying to sit next to a cranky statistician all game." She winks, then elbows her dad, who looks as if he wants to say something, but just shakes his head.

And I wonder, if D were here right now, what would he say?

He'd probably hit me with *Bro, not you crushing on the Coach's daughter? For real?* And he'd rub my head and say, *You tryna build a fire with gasoline, huh?* And I'd pretend to push him outta our seat. And we'd laugh until our eyes watered. Laughing until our stomachs hurt.

One hour later, according to my map app, we're less than forty-five minutes to the tournament site, and despite the 4:45 a.m. wake-up, I still haven't fallen asleep yet, alternating between staring at the charts and lists Kiara and I put together and staring out the window at the strange world passing by. I guess this is how everything looks when you're more miles from home than you've ever been—brand-new. Like driving through an alien world.

We zip past stretches where there's nothing but houses with front yards all lined up in a row, just houses and more houses, long driveways with cars and vans and bikes, some of the driveways empty.

People are mowing their lawn, sitting in their flower garden, pulling weeds.

People are checking their mailboxes.

People sitting on their porch reading, rocking back and forth on their porch swing.

I don't see any apartment buildings. Around OS, there are more apartments than houses; it's not even close.

Plus, the animals, everywhere. And not just cats and dogs. Nope. I'm clocking cows and pigs and horses. A few goats and a whole yard full of chickens.

Some weird-looking llama thing that Coach tells everyone to look at.

"It's an alpaca," he says.

"Al *who*?" J-Wu says, laughing.

"It looks like a hairy camel," Special K shouts from the back.

"Alpaca," Coach repeats.

Special K shrugs. "Sorry, Coach, but I know a hairy camel when I see one."

DJ aims his phone out the window and takes a picture. "Coach, we still in America, right?" he asks, shaking his head as we pass the largest barn I've ever seen. Okay, it's also the *only* barn I've ever seen, but still.

But then we pass even bigger barns with huge towers that look like rockets aimed at the sky, waiting to blast off. "They're called silos," Coach explains.

Every new building we see, I try to guess what's inside.

Hay? Corn? More alpacas?

It's weird when you think about it—how many doors there are in this whole world versus how many you actually ever walk through.

There are so many things we never see.

How many things would *I* never see? Tony, the kid who barely had two feet outside OS.

Tony, the kid whose most exciting place he's ever visited is the zoo back in third grade, except he kept getting in trouble because he asked the tour guides how would you like it if someone came and snatched you outta your real home and dropped you into some small cage for people to stare at you?

Tony versus the suburb kids at my school—how they come back from spring break talking about what they did at Disney World, what it was like riding a plane all the way up in the sky so that the world below was like an ant farm.

Tony talking about building snowmen in the middle of Paradise Court, versus the kids who come back from winter break talking about it never snows in Southern California.

Coach nods toward his window. "You see that?" Coach asks. "Just up ahead."

"What am I supposed to see, Coach?" I ask. "I don't see anything but cars, cars, and more cars. How many cars are there in—"

But then I see it—a shiny blue sign on the side of the road. Welcome to Illinois, it says.

Coach smiles at me, and I realize I'm still staring across the aisle, over his seat, and out his window—an extra-goofy, super-toothy smile on my face. I'm grinning so hard my cheeks hurt.

Kiara takes out an earbud and looks my way. "First time out of Wisconsin?"

I nod.

"Well, it won't be your last, Tony," Coach says, holding out his fist for me to tap. "You're going places, man."

"*We're* going places, Coach," I say, still nodding. "All of us."

## 24

### CHICAGO, ILLINOIS
#### 2 MONTHS TILL ORLANDO

Surprise: we get off to another slow start.

Except unlike last time, it's not for lack of heart.

We're playing hard. We're hustling and giving our all on defense.

The problem is, we can't knock down a shot to save our mamas' lives.

It's like there's a lid on our hoop they forgot to take off— every shot rims out.

We're even blowing wide-open layups. Kiara shoots me an *Is this really happening?* look from the baseline, where she's recording the game for the player reels. With two minutes left in the first quarter, we're down nine, and you can tell it's getting to us.

As if that wasn't bad enough, the Wolves (ranked the seventh-best team in the nation) led by their star player, Dre Lattimore (ranked as the number-four player in the nation), have been talking trash nonstop since tip-off.

*Yo, y'all need me to lift you little guys up to the rim, make it easier for you to throw up all those bricks?*

*The way I'm killing y'all, your coach gonna have to take y'all straight to the funeral home the minute this game's over. For real, your whole team's getting buried.*

*Please tell me I didn't just break your ankles in front of your people. Please tell me your grandma's not in the stands because that would make my stomach ache. No, wait, I think that was just the breakfast burrito I ate, my bad.*

On and on and on.

And that's just what I hear from the sideline.

"Guys are frustrated, Coach," I say.

"We're still in this game," Kiara says, sitting on the other side of me now.

"Basketball is a game of runs. We just gotta weather the storm," Coach says as KO beats his man to the rack with a hesitation dribble, only to leave the ball just short, rolling off the rim.

KO slaps his hands together and barks at the ref. "Yo, I'm getting killed in there! Call the foul!"

The ref ignores KO, but KO keeps complaining, even as Coach tells him to get back on defense. But by the time KO jogs to the other end of the court, the Wolves, playing five-on-four, are already laying the ball in.

Coach yells time-out, and the players huddle around him. "Listen," Coach says, clapping his hands. "Don't worry if it goes in or not. Just keep shooting. Eventually, they'll fall. Keep battling."

The team nods and returns to the floor, but Coach tells KO to hang back.

"Could a ref missing a foul call cost us the game? Maybe. But you not getting back on D? We *will* lose this game and every game after it. That can't happen again. If it does, you're gonna be picking bench splinters out of your butt, you got me?"

"But, Coach, they hacking me like I'm hibachi chicken out there. How am I s'pose to—"

Coach cuts in. "Let me handle the refs. You play. You wanna be the leader on this team? The best leaders don't *talk*. They *do*. We good?"

"Yeah," KO says, quietly between his teeth. "We good."

But three minutes into the second quarter, the ball still won't go through the hoop, and slowly our guys start to fade. "Stick to our game plan," Coach says, pumping his fists, clapping his hands, trying to rally everyone. "Be aggressive. We're still in this."

Here's the thing about us Sabres: everything about us is super aggressive.

On defense, we attack. We trap, blitz, and force turnovers.

On offense, we attack. We advance the ball quickly, spread

the floor, look for the transition layup or dunk; if it's not there, we swing the ball to the open shooter—and you give us even a semi-open look and it's *splash splash splash* all game.

So, yeah, a pretty good strategy that usually works, except when, you know, the other team is just as quick and plays sound, fundamental defense—

Then, suddenly, we're playing *their* game. We're playing their pace, their tempo. They've slowed us way down. Now we're not getting the open looks we're used to. Now we're not getting out on the break like we need to. Now there are fewer possessions, which means less opportunities to score.

Which is capital-T Trouble, because the truth is, we're not a great half-court team.

To be real, we're not even a *good* half-court team.

Not because we don't have the players to run half-court sets.

No, we've got plenty of perimeter firepower, plus we've got dominant low-post presence between Zay and Special K, working on the block. On paper, we should *dominate* the half-court.

But we don't because, well, our players are kind of, ummm, selfish.

So far, our favorite play to run is this:

1. We stop passing the ball around.

One player stands in place at the top of the key and dribbles.

That player keeps dribbling. Maybe between their legs or

behind their back.

Still dribbling.

2. Take an awful, super-contested shot that has maybe a 10 percent chance of going in.

Halfway through the second quarter, Coach actually sits for once.

"Well," he says.

And I look at him like *Well, what.*

"Any insights you wanna share? Patterns you've noticed?"

"Not yet," I say with a shrug. "But I'm working on it, Coach."

At halftime, we're down 33–17 to the Wolves, and it's feeling like déjà vu.

Coach James is mad, but he doesn't lose control. Instead, he stalks the locker room like a lion, not saying a word—which, hot take, is kinda worse than yelling.

*That's my dad*, Kiara said during the first quarter. *He's a quiet storm.* I wonder how Kiara's gonna put together a highlight reel without highlights.

"Look, I'm okay with missing shots and turnovers when we're being aggressive. But you guys are taking awful shots and forcing the action instead of letting the game come to you," Coach says, standing in front of the team.

And then Coach does something that I'm not expecting. "Now, Tony has noticed a few trends that are impacting our performance today, and he's gonna share a few of those notes. So, everyone, listen up."

"Oh," I say, pleading Coach with my eyes. "I thought me and Kiara . . . I thought we were just s'posed to tell *you* what we figure out, the numbers and stuff that, uh . . . you know . . . we collect . . . I—I didn't think I had to . . . do . . . uh . . . you know . . . *this*."

But Coach stands there, arms folded, and everyone's staring like they're at a theater and I'm the movie they're waiting to start playing. I swallow hard and stand up. "So, umm, yeah, like Coach said I've, uh, noticed a few things that I think, you know, if we . . ."

"Bro, you wanna speed this up? Halftime is only ten minutes," Meeks says. He's right. We don't have a lot of time, so I clear my throat and I get to it.

"The Wolves? They're winning because they're doing three things we aren't. One, they're sharing the ball, averaging three to four more passes per possession than us, and those extra passes have led to seven more field goals made."

I wait for someone to disagree. Coach nods, like *Keep going.*

"Two, they're playing disciplined defense. Us, not so much. Look, it's great to be aggressive with our traps, but our weakside rotation is trash. We're hedging. Six times we got caught in no-man's-land, guarding no one. The Wolves scored on five of those defensive lapses, so."

"What else?" DJ says. "You said *three* things."

There is one more thing, but it's gonna make a few players

mad, and one in particular.

"If it helps us win, we need to know, Tone," Coach says.

"So, uh, yeah, there's one more thing . . ." I pause and take a deep breath.

The locker room door flies open, and some random person pokes their head in and announces, "Yo, Coach, halftime's over. Y'all gotta get out there."

The players start for the door, but Coach stops them. "Let's hear that third thing Tone. You've got fifteen seconds."

I lift the paper up, my hand's shaking, but if I care about this team, I gotta do the hard things, too, right?

"We've got eleven turnovers in the first half alone," I hear myself say. "We've all been a little sloppy. But two players have hurt us the most . . ."

I feel the energy shift as everyone wonders the same thing: Is he really about to put the people we all know he's really talking about on blast?

"Meeks, you're one of our best ball handlers, but you had four turnovers. One was from you being aggressive—we can live with that. But the other three, you were over-dribbling. Last season, you averaged seven assists in AAU, but you've only got one right now, so."

Meeks frowns, takes a step toward me. "You think I'm why we're losing?"

I shake my head. "I think you're our point guard because you've got great court vision. There's probably no one in this tournament that sees the whole floor like you. We need *that* Meeks this second half." I swallow hard enough that I wonder if everyone else heard it.

But then Meeks nods. "Stat man's not wrong. That's my bad, guys. I can play better."

I almost smile, but then I remember, I'm not done. "KO, if not for your eleven points this might've been a blowout, but you've got six turnovers. I think if you—"

But KO gives me the finger. "Nah, son. Let me hit *you* with some stats. AAU teams *I've* made? Two. AAU teams *you've* made . . ." He holds up his hand in an O shape. "Zero, bruh. Zilch."

Coach cuts in. "Enough, KO. No one on this team is above criticism, me included."

"KO, it's no secret you're better than me. You're a leader on this team because of your talent. But true leadership is earned. You say you're the best, so be the best, then. Out there *and* in here."

KO's face is tight as a clenched fist, his forehead's creased, and his eyebrows are slanted like an angry emoji. "Yo, who is this guy?" KO says, laughing sharply. *"Be a leader, KO. We need you,"* he parrots me. A few guys laugh.

I clap my hands. "That's a great impression, man. You got me, ha." I fold my arms across my chest. "I hope the team can still laugh when your selfishness costs us this game."

"Ohhhh, snap, he went *in* on KO," Special K says, covering his mouth like he can't believe it.

KO takes a few angry strides toward me, but Meeks and

DJ step in his path before he reaches me. "D's not here to save you anymore. You're on your own now, little man. And spoiler alert, that's not gonna be a good look for you later, if you know what I mean."

Coach cuts in. "We don't make threats on this team."

KO laughs. "This team? It's like this punk said, *You don't win without me.*"

"Winning's not everything."

"Especially when you're a washed-up has-been," KO spits.

Anger and hurt flash on Coach's face like lightning. "Johnny, you're starting. KO, you're on the bench."

"You can't bench me! I'm the best player in this whole tournament. All these teams out here dying for me to ball with them. You think I need *you*? You think I need *this*?"

"Yo, chill, man, chill," Meeks says, grabbing KO by the arm. "C'mon, you're right, we need you. Let's just go get this W, and we'll all feel better."

But KO jerks away and storms out of the locker room, slamming the door so hard it bounces back open. The team follows him, and now it's just me and Coach.

"KO's a hothead," Coach says.

"Exactly, I was only telling the truth. I can't help it if—"

"But you went too far. Ball's emotional, but you let your emotions take over. You let your pride get the best of you. That's selfish, too."

I shake my head. "I'm sorry, Coach, but he tried to play

me in front of the team. I can't let that slide."

"Why can't you?"

"Because . . . because . . . then everybody thinks they can walk all over you and you'll just take it like a . . . like a . . . punk."

"Is that the worst thing that'll happen? People will think you're a punk?"

"You're acting like respect doesn't matter. You forget I'm from OS."

"*You* forget *I'm* from OS, too," Coach fires back.

It's quiet for a second, and then Coach sighs and his shoulders drop a little. "Tone, being tough isn't about being hard or mean. It's about not letting people rattle you. Not letting anyone get in your head and make you be something you're not. Toughness is in here," he says, tapping his head. "Respect is earned, but it takes time, when people learn they can trust you. You think the way you went at KO earned you this team's trust?"

"Coach, he's the one who—"

But Coach is already out, the door rocking behind him.

When I make it to our sideline, the game's thirty seconds in.

I walk past my spot, down to the far end of the bench.

KO's sitting in his warm-up jacket, DJ and Special K on either side. I crouch beside him, but he doesn't look my way. "KO, how things went down in the locker room," I say. "I was wrong to snap at you. I'm sorry, man."

KO's eyes stay on the court.

"Good luck," I say before heading down to the other end and taking my seat next to Coach. "My bad, Coach," I say loud enough for him to hear over the game noise. "You're right. I can't lose my cool. It won't happen again."

Coach's eyes stay on the court, but he holds out his fist and I tap it with mine.

I glance down at KO, and no, he's not smiling, but he looks less angry than before.

Maybe that's not a lot.

But it's not nothing.

We start the third with a 17–4 run.

Our first-half problems? Long gone. Everyone's pumped, including Coach, and as we watch our guys retake the floor after a time-out, he nudges me. "You see that, Tone? How they're leaning into each other and laughing?"

"Yeah, I think so."

"Body language tells you everything. First half, our guys didn't believe they could win, and they didn't believe in each other. But now . . ."

I shrug. "I guess winning cures everything, right?"

"Not everything, but this is a good start," Coach says, gesturing toward the end of the bench. "Yo, KO? You feeling dangerous?"

KO hops up and rips off his warm-up jacket. "Always," he says.

I stand up to meet him face-to-face, which is harder than

it sounds because he's got me by three or four inches.

"We good, bro?" I ask, extending my fist.

KO glances back at DJ and Special K. "Yo, y'all hear something?"

Special K shrugs, and DJ shakes his head. "C'mon, KO. The man apologized."

"Can we be cool for the team?" I ask.

But KO bumps into my outstretched hand, his long, easy strides getting him to the scorer's table quickly.

"I'm guessing that's a no," Special K says, barely fighting off a laugh.

I drop my un-dapped fist and retake my seat.

"That went well," I say to Coach.

He grins. "Ha, welcome to coaching, my brother."

I pick up my clipboard, and instantly my feelings fall away and my head's back in the game.

The fourth quarter's tight—we go back and forth, trading baskets with the Wolves—we take the lead, they take it back. Neither team pulls away.

Meeks is dribbling up top while Zay sets a hard screen to free up KO. It works—KO flashes to the wing with a good look at a corner three. Except KO's defender recovers enough to block KO's shot, or at least make KO think twice about releasing.

KO's jumper is as quick as it is beautiful, and he releases the ball over the defender's outstretched hand. The shot falls cleanly through the net.

With less than a minute left, we're up two.

But the Wolves surprise us. All game, they've played slower than sleepy, but now they push the ball, running a double screen on the baseline that wipes out J-Wu, and zipping the ball around the perimeter—*zzzp zzzp zzp*—faster than we can rotate. Zay closes fast, but he's a split second late, and the Wolves' leading scorer, Trash-Talk Dre, nails a clutch three to reclaim the lead.

Zay taps his chest, like *my bad*, hangs his head as he jogs up the court.

"Keep your head up, Zay," I yell in his direction. "We need you right here."

On cue, the ball swings Zay's way; Zay feeds the post with

153

a perfect loft pass down to Meeks. Meeks pivots left, looking for a diving J-Wu underneath the rim, but J-Wu slips and the pass isn't there, so Meeks hits Zay at the top of the key. Zay looks for KO to get open, but they're double-teaming KO, two Wolves defenders sandwiching him.

"Time-out," Coach yells. We huddle up. I glance at the scoreboard.

"We're one basket and one defensive stop away from

completing this comeback."

"Coach, I got this. If somebody can get me the ball." KO shoots Zay a look, and Zay shrugs.

"I try to force the action to you, KO, and that's an easy steal. Whole reason we're in this game is because of what Coach and Tone said. We're taking care of the rock. You're my boy, but I'm not about to force-feed you and cost us the game, bruh, sorry. *We've all* worked too hard."

And everyone's surprised because Zay's more the silent type—but he's right.

KO sees it differently. "Whatever. Coach, just run that same double screen they ran on us, and I'll get the shot off, trust me. I'mma make all y'all look good."

Coach shakes his head. "No hero ball, KO. We win or

lose as a team. If you beat your man off the dribble, do what you do. But if they trap, kick it to Zay for a midrange."

"Bump that. A contested jumper from me is better than Zay's wide-open midrange. We all know that."

Coach's voice booms. "You wanna sit this play out, KO?"

KO shrugs. "What? Did I lie?"

I clear my throat. "We should run that play, but on the rub when both defenders follow KO expecting him to take the shot, he hits Zay in the corner. If the shot's there, take it, like Coach said. But if not, look for that crosscourt pass to Meeks in the corner. It's gonna be wide open, since Meeks's man is helping on their traps."

KO shakes his head. "Wait. You wanna use me as a decoy? Is you for real? Yo, why are we even listening to this scrub?"

"Tone's right," Meeks says. "They're leaving me to help on you every time. I've been wide open, but you're not seeing me."

"No, I see you. I just see me being better, so."

"This ain't about you," Zay says, stepping to KO. "It's team or nothing. Sabres over everything. You either with us or you against us. What's it gonna be?"

Coach cups his hand on Zay's shoulder. "Zay, you're the first option after KO draws the double. Otherwise, skip over to Meeks."

Zay and Meeks nod, and Coach puts his hand in the middle of all of us, Black side up, palm down. "Good. One huddle, one hustle, one head, one heart."

For a sec, KO looks like he may not go back in the game, the other four already on the court and in position. But then KO walks to his spot. And I wonder if he's gonna run the play or try to be a hero.

It wouldn't be the first time KO did KO.

Special K looks to inbound the ball. The Wolves are grabbing and holding us, making it hard to receive Special K's pass.

Coach is jumping up and down, yelling, "Hit Meeks! Hit Meeks!"

Special K tries to bounce pass to Meeks, but the ball ricochets off Meeks's shoe and sails out of bounds. The good news is it glances off a Wolves player first.

"We're out of time-outs, yeah?" Coach asks the ref.

"Yeah, Coach," the ref replies.

Coach turns back to Special K. "Don't bounce it. Keep it in the air. Use your height, big man."

This time, Special K's pass is better but still off the mark, nearly sailing past Meeks into the backcourt, but Meeks is able to corral it. KO's racing to the ball for the handoff, and just like we predicted, the Wolves send a second defender.

KO dribbles hard to avoid the trap and for a moment it seems he's successful, but the second defender cuts him off, leaving KO with two options:

A. Stick to the plan and dish to Zay, or

B. Say *forget y'all* and take an off-balanced jumper over two, maybe three defenders.

It's clear the Wolves are selling out to guard KO. They're not gonna let him beat them.

But KO's got that look in his eyes, that *you can't stop me, not now, not ever* stare as he dribbles through his legs enough to throw the second defender off balance. The primary defender tries to crowd KO's off hand, playing him for the crossover, but KO's got other magic up his sleeve—aiming the ball between defender #1's legs.

KO drops the ball between Trash-Talk Dre's legs, and the crowd goes crazy, cheering, oohing and aahing, and I'm pretty sure I catch a smile flash on KO's face.

Because, yep, he left Trash-Talk Dre looking silly—and now KO's got an open lane to the rack. The Wolves big man rotates into the paint, sliding his feet to cut KO off or take the charge. Everyone in the gym knows KO's taking this shot—

This is what KO lives for. These moments. The big lights. The glory.

The seconds tick off as KO leaves his feet, elevating for the rim, the Wolves center leaping to challenge KO's shot. With three seconds left, the ball leaves KO's hands . . . and . . . wait, the ball . . . it's going the wrong way, it's going . . .

It's going . . .

To Meeks all alone in the corner, the ball delivered on time so that Meeks doesn't even have to make an adjustment, just catch and shoot in rhythm, and Meeks's jump shot is a thing of beauty, it's a perfect burnt-orange sphere arcing up up up in slow motion, a rainbow headed right for the rim. The crowd suddenly quiet and on their feet, waiting to erupt in a victorious cheer.

And the ball slides gracefully into the rim, kissing the net as it cyclones toward the bottom.

Except it doesn't fall through the nylon. No, it spins inside, dancing, whirling, corkscrewing, ping-ponging, doing everything but dropping dropping until—

*Bladah doop!*

It pops out the top—like the net changed its mind, the rim spitting it out hard as the final buzzer sounds.

"Wait, that went in, right?" J-Wu says quietly. "It fell in, yeah?"

I shake my head. "How did that *not* fall?"

"Told ya'll can't hang with us. Y'all better hope you never see us again. We own your sorry team," Trash-Talk Dre shouts as the Wolves explode in celebration, pumping their arms, jumping up and down, hugging each other—while the Sabres slink over back to the bench, untucking their jerseys, not making eye contact with each other.

Another hard loss. And I don't know—is it better to lose in a blowout, or lose a close game at the buzzer?

"Now that was a game," Coach says, clapping his hands in admiration. "You were down by nineteen—"

Kiara cuts in. "Twenty-three!"

"Twenty-three points and you lost by one. That was one of the gutsiest performances I've seen in a while. I'm proud of you. You never quit. You dug deep, and you believed in each other. And I won't lie—I don't believe in moral victories. We'd all rather be celebrating a win right now, *but* . . . I've never been prouder after a loss. I'm proud of each one of you."

And you can feel it—everyone's spirit lifting a bit.

Well, almost everyone. Meeks hasn't lifted his head since his shot rimmed out.

"Hey, man, don't beat yourself up, Meeks," I say. "Nine times out of ten that balls falls in and we win the game."

Coach taps KO on the shoulders. "Everyone did what they were supposed to."

KO wags his head. "No, we didn't. I should've shot it," KO says. "Game on the line, I'm the only one cold enough to hit that winner. Facts."

Meeks drapes a towel over his shoulders and walks away.

"Meeks, wait up, man," DJ calls, chasing after him.

"KO, you made the right basketball play. And if we find ourselves in those same circumstances, I expect you to make the right play again."

"You still not gonna admit you was wrong, huh? Ain't that what you preach, Coach? So admit it. You wish I'd taken it."

"Why didn't you, then?" Coach fires back a bit harder than I think he wanted.

"Because from now on, I don't wanna hear nobody's mouth about who's the man and who's not."

Coach shakes his head. "You passed because you didn't want your shot sent to the moon. And because you knew Meeks gave us the best chance to win."

KO laughs. "Bro, you need your eyes checked. And maybe your head, too, for even thinking you could win without me making it happen."

"Careful, KO. We're all competitors here. We hate to lose and sometimes we say things we don't mean, but you're one word away from—"

KO steps close enough to bump Coach. It's in this moment I realize how big KO is. He's not as tall as Coach, but he's big enough to make most grown men think twice.

"I'm one word from *what*?" KO says, spitting the words like venom. Like a snake about to strike.

Coach squares his shoulders. "I strongly suggest you step back, young man."

But KO inches closer, so now he's nose to nose. KO's arm wheels back, and I can't believe this is happening. Is he really about to swing on Coach James?

We'll never know because DJ and Special K pull him back, but he yanks away. "Get your hands off me, scrubs! Bunch of losers. Y'all can't lace my Nikes. What, you think I *need* this wack team? You got any idea how many teams constantly hit me up, begging me to run with them? Telling me I'm crazy to stay here, but I'm like, nah, I wanna rep my hood, my city. But this . . . this is trash. Y'all don't like how I play, what I do for this team, let's see how you do without me."

"KO," I say. "Please don't . . ."

"Yo, why are you even talking? You shouldn't even be here. But since you are . . ." KO grabs the bottom of his jersey and pulls it up over his head, throws it hard into my face, his sweat stinging my eyes. "You can do my laundry, punk. Matter of fact, I got some dirty draws for you, too."

But then Zay steps up and then Special K and J-Wu, forming a wall between me and KO.

"Maybe you should just go, KO, you hate it here so much," J-Wu says.

"No one's stopping you," Special K adds with a shrug.

KO looks shocked. "That what y'all really want? Y'all better think long and hard because, once I'm gone, there ain't enough begging on the planet that'll bring me back."

And no one says *leave*. But also no one says *stay*.

KO laughs. "Y'all seriously gonna regret this. I'mma personally make sure of it, watch. Bump this trash team and this bum coach. And you, don't worry," he says glaring at me, while he tugs on his drawstring and loosens his shorts. "I'll make sure you get these draws. I know where you stay."

Coach's nostrils flare. "You threaten another one of my players and—"

KO holds up his hands as he turns to walk away. "I'll be seeing y'all. Or should I say, y'all will be seeing me." He swivels back, his eyes fiery, his grin wicked—that *cat ate the canary* face, Big Mama calls it. "In your nightmares. Catch y'all in Orlando for the chip. If you still make it."

# 25

The protest starts at Ellison Avenue, and I can't tell how many people show up, but it's more than were at the community meeting. Everyone's here—the Sabres squad, everybody from OS, and people from nearby communities. There are even folks who drove from other states here. I wish I could fly because I'd swoop high above our heads, staring down at this mass of friends and strangers, all of us marching as one for over two miles, sing-shouting in unison, *We demand justice. Justice for Dante* the entire way. I keep looking down at Tasha, waiting for her to get tired, to complain her feet hurt, but she's pumping her fist and shouting right along with us.

Dad called off work to be here, which maybe seems like a small thing, but Dad *never* misses work. Like, Mom jokes that when she was in labor with Tasha, she threatened that if Dad didn't leave work and get to the hospital right away, he should find some other place to live. It's that serious. But here he is, waving A Real Justice, Right Now sign written in his handwriting—me, Tasha, Munka, and Big Mama walking in lockstep beside him.

Finally, the marching comes to a stop in front of the main police precinct, which is conveniently right next to the mayor's office. Standing in a straight line, blocking the stone steps to the police station, are at least fifty armed officers rocking riot gear and serious faces.

"Go home," a few officers snap. "This isn't gonna change a thing."

But we don't go home. We keep chanting. We keep shouting. We keep demanding justice.

Soon there are news trucks, local and one or two national reporters, swarming our protest, sticking mics in protestors' faces and asking why they feel it's important to be here—and everyone answers nearly the same exact way:

*Because a life was needlessly taken and we're tired of losing. We're tired of RIP hashtags. We're tired of burying our family and friends. We're tired of justice being for everyone but us.*

*But do you think any of this will change anything?* the reporters press.

*It has to. Something has to change.*

There must be four hundred candles lit all around the edge of Paradise Court. It's hard to say what D would've wanted us to do in the wake of his death. I know he wouldn't want us to be sad or in pain or angry enough to hurt anyone else.

But I feel like he'd love this.

The soft orange glow of so many candles dancing in the light evening breeze.

I wondered if after the protest people would go home, but nope, everyone's still here, still united.

Some people cry, even as they hug each other. Some people stand on crates and talk about how God's taking care of Dante, keeping him safe . . .

Zay shakes his head. "Are they trying to tell us there are basketball hoops in heaven?"

And we laugh, which feels weird, laughing near the place that makes me the saddest. But I don't know—I guess being here with so many other people who D meant something to makes it easier to walk across the asphalt.

Some people put photos of D in the spot where he took his last breath, others place stuffed animals and bundles of flowers from their gardens, and someone even brings a box of D's favorite candy and sets it right there on that spot.

"I wish Mom was here," I say to Munka. "She always knows what to say. What to do."

Munka nods. "Me too," she says, squeezing my arm almost how Mom always does, as if something as small and as quick as an arm squeeze is a way to tell someone you love them. And no, it's not exactly a Mom squeeze, but it's not the worst thing, either.

At one point, we all join hands and share what we miss most about D—

But then someone says something I'll never forget.

That when we say *I miss the way D laughed with his whole body*, we're really saying *I loved the way D laughed.* And that missing someone and loving them are two cords tied together.

Yes, it's okay to miss D, but remembering that I miss him because I love him, I don't know, I guess it sorta makes it a little less sad.

And any less sadness is a good start.

# 26

## INDIANAPOLIS, INDIANA

Without KO, I can't even lie, the rest of our games are wild shaky.

It's like when he left the team, he also left this KO-sized hole in the middle of us, a hole only he can fill. And now, if we're gonna win, everyone's gotta do more, stepping into roles they weren't ready for. *Next man up,* Coach keeps preaching. "The Sabres aren't one player," he says. "We're a team. One huddle, one hustle, one head, one heart."

We lose the first Life After KO game by nine.

But the next game, down seven with three minutes to go, we rally for our first win of the season. All of us erupting in cheers and hollering like we just won game seven of the NBA Finals.

We wrap up the Indy tournament at 3–2, falling just short of the playoff rounds.

So, are we good with how things are going?

No way.

But after starting 0–2, we strung together three consecutive wins by an average of eleven points. Not bad considering we haven't played a lot of road games together.

The bus roars to life, but Coach pops up from his seat, clearing his throat. "Listen, all that matters is right now," he says, pointing his finger at the floor. "We can't change the past. All that matters are the humans on this bus. If we take care of each other, if we respect this game, if we remember to have fun, I promise you, the wins will come."

Coach's eyes sweep across every single face. "One huddle, one hustle, one head, one heart."

And we shout it right back. "One huddle, one hustle, one head, one heart!"

There are six or seven cars waiting in the Bray parking lot.

I spot Big Mama's right away, mainly because she's got her head poked out the window and she's waving like we've been gone for months instead of all day.

I say goodbye to the team, wave to Coach and Kiara, and slide into the front seat of Big Mama's car. Munka taps me on my head, whispers, *Good job, little bro*; Tasha's asleep on

Munka's shoulder in the back seat.

"I think I see why you've been so happy lately, Tony," Big Mama says, looking out her window, telling Coach thank you and asking about the *pretty girl* with him.

"No offense, Coach," Big Mama tells him. "But she obviously got her mom's looks."

But Coach just laughs. "Thank God."

And I'm so happy for the first time in forever that it doesn't even faze me when Munka leans into the front seat to sing, *Tony's got a girlfriend, Tony's got a girlfriend.*

I mean, hey, there are worse songs.

And I guess I'm finally ready to sleep, too, because as I'm wondering what coming home will feel like when we're actually winning the way we can, the way we should, imagining how many cars might be waiting for us then, my eyes are growing heavier and heavier and I can't say for sure but I'm pretty sure I'm snoring before we're even out of the parking lot.


Munka carries Tasha upstairs to bed, and I start to follow after them, but Big Mama calls me back down.

"I didn't want to say this in front of Tasha, in case she woke up," Big Mama says, a worried look on her face. "Officer Truman . . ." She reaches out and takes my hand. "End of the month, they're letting him go back to work and they're not gonna change his assignment."

"Wait, for real? I thought that with all the bad press,

they'd charge him this time."

Big Mama shakes her head but no words come out, so I keep going. "So, what, Terry gets locked up for threatening Truman, but Truman actually kills D and he gets a paid vacation? He gets to stroll back into OS, walking around like all that pain he caused ain't ever happen? He gets to yell at us *to get over here* or *empty your pockets now* same as always? Push us against those brick walls, pat us down? Put his hands all over us, throw us to the ground? Same way he did D? Like D's life ain't matter?"

Big Mama tries to hug me, but I can't. "No!" I hear myself yell.

Because I'm tired of everyone acting like every bad thing can be fixed with hugs. I'm tired of adults telling *you* to do the right thing, telling *you* to make good choices, promising you that if you do everything right it will all be fine.

Because in the end, all the good you do in this world can't stop the bad things from coming.

And all the trouble you work so hard to avoid doesn't keep the trouble from coming after you.

Because being good doesn't make you bulletproof.

# 3RD QUARTER

When D was here, I lived for ball.

If you asked me if I loved it as much as he did, I would've said yeah. But now, looking back, I'm not sure. I *liked* ball, but I think the thing I loved was being around D.

He didn't treat me like a kid. He never said, *You're too small.* He didn't put his game first, as if I was only there to help him. And sometimes it was all he could talk about.

We talked about the Bucks games.

We debated which college conference produced the best NBA players.

We broke down x's and o's, which is a fancy way of saying *strategy.*

Like, how to attack a box-and-1 defense. Or how to front the post, making it harder for your opponent to pass the ball down to their bigs.

I don't know if I know anyone who loved anything as much as D loved ball. I'd get a text in the middle of the night, like *Bro, tomorrow we gotta practice blocking out for rebounds.* And then he'd send like a dozen smiling emojis because that's how ball made him feel.

It's like when your friend has a cold, you gotta stay away or you're gonna get sick. D loved ball so much, it was contagious. Like, how could I *not* catch it?

And then he literally died on the court, and now it's this strange thing where it's the last place I wanna be because it reminds me of him. But also it's the only place I wanna be because it reminds me of him. Which is like saying I'm hot and cold at the same time. Like, *what?*

Life's weird, man. That two completely opposite things can both be true.

And yeah, I wanted to make the team because I wanted to make him proud. Because ball was important to him. It was our thing.

But now it's like I'm falling in love with ball all over again.

Or maybe more like for the first time, on my own, because it matters to me, too.

Because it reminds me, *I* matter.

Suddenly, for weeks now, all I do is eat, sleep, and dream basketball.

Okay, yes, sometimes, *occasionally*, Kiara sneaks in there, too, but like, not *that* much. I mean, I'm not sprung.

The point is, I'll probably never have half of D's talent. Maybe one day KO will be on TV shaking hands with the commissioner at the NBA Draft and I'll be watching at home on my couch. And that's okay. Other ways to win.

Who knows—maybe KO makes it to the league and I'm that team's statistician?

And then an assistant coach.

A head coach.

A general manager of an entire team.

The president of basketball operations.

Because there's not just one way to do a thing. Because there's more than one way to win.

"I've got an announcement," Coach says to the team, out of nowhere—and not gonna lie, for a second I think he's gonna tell us Terry's getting released.

It's not fair, how they still won't let us see him, other than Aunt Tracy.

*What are they trying to hide, keeping that boy locked up like this?* Big Mama says every other day, as if she's saying it brand-new for the first time.

Except the distance between any news about Terry and what Coach actually tells us is roughly the same distance apart as Mercury is from Neptune.

Coach clears his throat. "These game trips shouldn't just

be about basketball. They're also opportunities for the team to explore new cities, new foods, architecture, and history. A chance for us all to experience the different ways other people live. A reminder that there are so many options when it comes to what we do with our lives. That we can play ball, sure, but we can also be artists or write comics or—"

"Design video games!" Special K shouts.

Everyone laughs, even Coach. "That's what I'm talking about! People always saying you gotta think outside the box, but nobody ever wants to show you how to get out of the box, or all the options you have once you're outside." Coach's voice softens. "For a lot of us, these tournament trips are the only times we've traveled out of the city or out of state. But this is only the beginning. We're all gonna get to see that we have the right and the power to dream bigger. That there's so much more to life than what we've been taught. Than what we've seen with our eyes."

And everyone's mad quiet, like how before a big storm, the wind is barely moving, the sky is still—but then, *boom*, rain and wind come swooshing down.

"Appreciate you, Coach," Zay says. "Thank you for, uh, you know . . . showing up. And caring about us even though you don't have to."

Coach nods his head, and I can't be sure, but the corners of his eyes look wetter than usual.

"Thanks, Coach," J-Wu chimes.

"Yeah, Coach, good looking out," Meeks says.

"One of the assistant coaches I played for at college always said this one thing that's sort of stuck with me. He said, *If these kids saw how big the world really is, maybe they'd understand how big they can be, too.* So that's what we're gonna do, together. We're gonna find out how big every single one of us can be."

Later, before everyone goes their separate ways, Coach calls me and Kiara over, a big smile on his face. Kiara shakes her head.

"Tony, we should probably run now, while we still can," she says.

I laugh. "What's up?"

"This is his *I'm gonna ask you to do something but you can't say no even if you want to* face," Kiara explains.

Coach, still grinning, folds his arms across his chest and shakes his head. "You think you know me or something?"

Kiara shrugs. *"Dad."*

"So you know how I just told the team we're gonna use these road trips to expand our minds and grow and all of that? What I meant was, me and the two of you are gonna scout the tournament cities ahead of time."

Kiara laughs. "But mainly, this is me and Tony's job, right? Am I reading between the lines well enough?"

"Girl, sometimes you're so like your mama, it's scary. But, uh, no, I'm definitely gonna help, but you know, if you and Tony wanna take the lead in scouting what there is to do in each of the tournament cities ahead of time, and then make a list of activities that the team can vote on, I mean, I won't try and stop you . . ."

"Told you, Tony," Kiara says.

But it doesn't even bother me.

### BALTIMORE, MARYLAND
#### 44 DAYS TILL ORLANDO

Coach is all, *Don't overpack*, but it happens, anyway.

Everyone shows up at the bus with their massive, borrowed-from-somebody suitcase.

I followed Big Mama up to the attic, helped her move old furniture and moving boxes and clothing racks around until we found what she was looking for.

A large suitcase that was in great shape but also kinda ancient.

Did she really want me to rock *this bag*?

But then, as she dusted it and unzipped the thick gold zipper, she smiled and looked up at me with watery eyes: *This belonged to your grandfather*, she said. *See*, she said, showing me three letters next to the handle—

And honestly, after that, it didn't matter if it was covered in pink flowers, I was sold.

And as I put everything inside, I imagined my grandfather—the shiny gold tooth in the front of his smile, the way he didn't walk but glided. *This is how you strut*, he used to say. *You watching me, Tony, watch your Papo move,* his big, airy laugh filling every room, like packing peanuts.

I carry the bag into the airport—my first time inside one—and I strut through security, all the way to the gate, and onto the plane. *Watch me move, Papo,* I say to myself. *Watch me move, Mom and Dad. Watch me move, D. Watch me.*

Every game is close.

Our biggest victory is only by four points, and two of our six games are decided by two points or less. But you can see it happening, you can see what we're building like how a mound of dirt on a construction site eventually becomes a building. That's us, we're getting stronger, we're trusting each other, and we're stacking wins.

In our toughest matchup, against the Detroit Roses, with forty seconds left on the clock, Zay uses his long arms to poke the ball away from the dribbler, dives for the loose ball, and tosses it ahead to a streaking Meeks—except the pass is too strong and headed out of bounds. But Meeks switches into another gear, his legs and arms pumping as fast as I've ever seen him move—knowing his momentum will carry him off the court and into the bleachers, he reaches out a split second before stepping out, grazing enough leather to keep the ball alive. Then DJ, who's almost always in the right place at the right time, scoops the rock and lays the ball in just as the ref calls time.

"Nope, that doesn't count. He didn't get it off in time," the Detroit coach shouts.

"Basket's good," the ref says. "Sabres win."

And we go wild. Jumping on Zay's back, tackling Meeks, mobbing DJ, until we're one big happy pile of knees and elbows and sweat.

"Y'all some fools," Coach says before diving in with us.

And just like that our record improves: *five wins, two losses.*

Back at the hotel, everyone's so exhausted, they plead for a "chill night" in.

But Coach looks at Kiara, then me—and in his big baritone voice says: "Gentlemen, basketball isn't only about winning *on* the court. Basketball is a tool that, if used properly, will help you win *off* the court, too."

"You're talking about the ladies, right, Coach?" Special K says, cheesing. "Shoot, y'all know how I do. The girls *especially* love Special K, ha." He and Zay fist-bump, and everyone laughs because it's funny, yeah, but also cuz we've all seen Special K in action—or more like, *in*action.

"Son, I know you're not talking about *you*, right? You *must* be talking cereal, yeah? Because I love that stuff, too. Had a big bowl this morning, in fact," Coach says, grinning.

Everyone cracks up again.

"Wow, Coach, you really gonna play me like that?" Special K asks, shaking his head.

"Man, Special K got less game than an empty gym," J-Wu chimes.

"Ha, even Tony got more game than Special K," Meeks says. "No offense, Tony," he adds, winking at me. And now we all really lose it, even me. Because he's right. I *don't* have game. But it's cool to know I'm not at the *very* bottom, haha.

Coach waits for the laughs to die down, and then he says, "I know you all wanna chill, but first we've got a few things to do."

"I already know what I'm tryna do, Coach," Special K says. "I'm tryna get at some fools in *NBA 2K* real quick. Who wanna get run? Huh?"

Zay shakes his head. "You already know you don't want it from me and DJ. Tell these scrubs, DJ."

DJ grins. "I mean, last time we played, I'm pretty sure Zay and I ain't never give up our controllers, so."

"Oh, so y'all tryna run twos?" Johnny asks.

"Heck yeah," Zay replies.

"Bet," Special K says, him and Johnny slapping five, like *You know we got this in the bag.*

And they probably would've gone on forever if Coach hadn't cut in again. "Ahem," Coach says, clearing his throat. "As I was saying, *first* we explore, *then* all y'all can get in line to catch an L from your coach."

Boos and cheers erupt from everyone. "Coach be cheating, though. He always tryna play with the All-Star teams," Meeks snaps.

But Coach shrugs. "That's because I wanna play on the team I was on, ha."

And no one can say anything to this except nod.

"So, Coach," Special K pipes up. "What we exploring?"

When Coach tells everyone to hit the shower and be in the lobby by one o'clock, we have no clue why. It's not until the whole team's walking outside and sees a man with a sign in his hands that reads Oasis Springs Sabres with a fancy shiny black bus behind him, waiting for us to board, that we realize just how seriously Coach James had taken our suggestion.

Thirty minutes later, we're standing outside the James E. Lewis Museum of Art. A few of the guys protest—*A museum, Coach, really?*—but Coach makes everyone promise to give it a *real* chance before we decide it's stupid.

Now, I'm not gonna pretend to know much about this destination because it was Kiara who'd placed it on our list, but what little she showed me about it ahead of time was enough to make me curious. And turns out, it's better than anything she could've said.

Our tour guide, Janelle, is pretty great too; a college junior Black girl with big eyes and a small 'fro—*Don't you love when women wear natural hair?* Kiara says to me at one point during the tour, and I nod even though I'm not 100 percent sure what that means.

Kiara asks Janelle lots of questions about the museum and about college—oh yeah, the museum's on the Morgan State University campus, which is also the largest of Maryland's

HBCUs—historically Black college and universities. It's cool if you didn't know what that meant—only a couple of guys on the team did, and I wasn't one of them.

There are so many cool art exhibits to see—everyone finds something they like. Kiara's really into Elizabeth Catlett's work, an artist who tried to bring attention to important women's issues. Me, I really dig the sculptures, especially Chakaia Booker's—I didn't even know you could make art out of rubber tires and scraps of metal, but her work's pretty dope.

"I wanna do something like this, Coach," I say.

He grins. "You can," he says back.

Says it like he believes it.

Like he means it.

## HOUSTON, TEXAS
### 36 DAYS TILL ORLANDO

We rattle off four easy wins to start the Houston tournament.

But the biggest surprise came at the airport *before* we boarded for Texas.

"Hi, guys, hope it's cool I tag along," Mrs. James said, stepping out from behind Coach James's six-foot-eight body and waving.

Three stats about Mrs. James:

She's a legit five foot nine, five foot ten, so . . . tall.

She played college ball at Arizona and was probably a WNBA lottery pick until she blew out her knee *twice*.

She's a sports medicine physician. She helps athletes stay healthy or recover from injuries. Right now, she's working at Marquette University, as a team doctor.

And okay, maybe this is weird to say—but I see where Kiara gets her smile from.

"Is it me or is Coach's wife kinda fire?" Special K whispers to me and Zay.

Zay nods. "*And* crazy smart. No cap, if you didn't have enough reasons to try and make the League *before*, you definitely got one now. Coach hit the lottery twice, haha."

Special K rotates his shoulder. "I might have to ask her for some medical attention on this shoulder, you feel me?"

We're cracking up, elbowing each other, until Coach *and* Kiara both shoot us looks, like *We know who you're talking about*, and we quickly turn the other way.

"Coach about to cut y'all minutes, watch," I say, still laughing.

"Or just cut us, period," Zay says, cheesing.

"Nah." Special K waves me off. "Not if you show him some numbers saying the team's more"—Special K switches on his *super-nerd voice*—"*efficient* with me and Zay on the court, he won't, *Mr. Calculator*."

And okay, he got me with that one.

When our Saturday games are over, Kiara and I ask to hang at the gym to scout a few of the other good teams still playing.

"You're really taking this seriously," Coach says, nodding.

"Keep up the good work."

Kiara walks around the court, recording the games from all angles, recording the coaches signaling in plays to their teams, while I sit near the top of the bleachers, scribbling notes like:

> *100% of the time, they trap off a made basket.*
>
> *They go one-on-one, relying on their size or athleticism 60% of the time versus running a designed play.*

In between games, Kiara sits next to me, and we compare notes.

I remember the first time I tried to read her handwriting. *Umm, what in the world is that?* I said, laughing. And she pretended to frown and said, *Leave my chicken scratch alone.*

I stick my hand in my pocket, feel the three folded twenty-dollar bills inside, the cash that Big Mama gave me for spending money. I decide to buy Kiara her favorite drink—some kind of fancy water—*seltzer*, I think she called it. All I know is that it has mad bubbles that I didn't expect and it tastes like somebody forgot to add flavor to the soda, but Kiara loves it and I don't know—she knows way more stuff about way more stuff than me.

Like, how to: *fold your clothes so you maximize your suitcase space*. And even though my luggage next to hers is old and less fancy—Kiara tells me how much she loves the pattern on my overnight bag.

How to: order room service. That you leave the dishes on the tray in the hallway, instead of being like me and walking it down to the front desk and asking where the kitchen was. The lady at the front desk just smiled and smiled; *Just leave it here, baby*, she said.

How to: ask for a blanket and pillow on the plane—Kiara didn't even laugh at me when I asked who did all that laundry for the plane, she just grinned and said, *You're fun, Tony. I like your brain.*

And if I smile any wider, my cheeks are gonna fall off the sides of my face.

It's just that no one's ever said anything like that to me. Well, I guess Big Mama, Mom, and Dad kinda have, but they're family. With Kiara, it hits different.

Maybe what Kiara knows most, though, is how to be confident. I'm not saying I have *zero* confidence since D died, but sometimes I feel a little shaky.

Kiara, though, *that girl* knows *she knows her stuff,* Big Mama said, officially meeting Kiara after practice a few weeks back. *I love her energy.*

Except Kiara and I aren't *exactly* alone—because while Coach and the team head back to the hotel for video games and burgers, Mrs. James hangs back to keep us company.

I gotta admit, hanging out with Mrs. James is pretty fun. She kinda reminds me of Mom, actually. Like, if Mom was here, she'd be making us laugh, telling jokes about Dad and telling us stories from when she was a kid—like Mrs. James is doing now.

After we gather intel on tomorrow's opponents—*the Cali*

*All-Stars love to trap and press; the Portland Infernos run their offense through the post*—Mrs. James orders a car to pick us up. But we drive two blocks past the hotel, stopping at a place called Hazel's.

"Ohmigod, Mom, root beer floats!" Kiara screams, clapping her hands together. Kiara turns to me, smiling wide. "Ohmigod, Tony, you're about to go crazy when you taste this ice cream. It's the *best*."

"But dinner first," Mrs. James says, holding the door open for me and Kiara to enter.

And it's wild—being with people I barely knew a few weeks ago but now feeling like I've known them forever.

And it's wild—being so far from OS—1,184 miles, our plane ticket said, starting to realize just how big the world really is. But also feeling like I can dream bigger, too. Feeling like *I'm* bigger.

# 30

The hotel phone rings, scaring the snot outta me.

Meanwhile, DJ and J-Wu don't even flinch. I remember when that used to be me, ha—DJ snoring louder than two people by himself and J-Wu canceling all that noise with his earbuds—so, yeah, I'm the only one who nearly falls outta bed.

Well, actually outta *chair*.

Because apparently, I fell asleep watching the video Kiara sent me after dinner.

"Downstairs in twenty," the voice on the phone says.

By the time I get ready, my twenty minutes are about up, so I don't even wait for the elevator. I hit the stairs and fly down the five flights.

I burst into the lobby, a little winded, and Coach is standing there in his tracksuit, reading a newspaper. He doesn't look up, just says, "Good morning, Tone."

I grumble the same back to him, my breath hot and sticky still even though I brushed and gargled. I hear Dad's voice in my head—*Better make sure you floss, Tony. That's how you really take care of your teeth—flossing.* But this is what happens when Coach wakes me up at six in the morning. "Everything okay, Coach?" I ask as the elevator door chimes and opens behind me.

"Morning, baby," Coach says, and I turn around to find Kiara stepping off the elevator.

"Good morning, guys," Kiara says, somehow smiling vibrantly even though it's way too early to be so happy. "Y'all ready to go over these game notes?"

Coach shakes his head, wipes his eyes. "I can't believe *you're* calling meetings now."

I look at Kiara. "You called this meeting?"

Kiara jabs Coach in the ribs. "Hey, you created this gym rat, Dad. Now you gotta live with the consequences."

Over orange juice and fancy oatmeal, we talk strategy, filling in Coach on everything we learned about our competition the evening before. Coach listens carefully and tells us what he likes about our suggestions and teaches us a box-and-1 defense. "We'll use this against the Infernos," he says. And it's pretty cool—I'm not stupid, I know Coach doesn't *need* me to scout for him, to be his statistician. Hello, he played in the League! He was a four-time All-Star! But here he is, smashing oatmeal and sipping juice, listening to me and his daughter talk 2-1-2 zones. It doesn't feel real.

But I guess that's sorta the vibe these days—things feeling unreal.

D's death.

Terry's arrest.

The whole world upside down.

The Cali All-Stars are just as talented as us—maybe even more.

But it's just like we scouted—they're so used to dominating with their athleticism, they don't bother playing fundamental ball. We outwork and outhustle them and win by nine.

And the Infernos? We light them up inside the paint, Special K leading the charge down low while Zay locks down their most explosive player, and yep, the Infernos go down in flames.

I'm sorry—I couldn't resist.

Later in our hotel room, Kiara and I are FaceTiming, watching some film on the four remaining teams in the tourney, when Special K leaps onto my bed, jumping up and down. I nearly drop my laptop.

"Bro, what are you doing?"

"It's on now," Special K says, smiling hard.

"What are you talking about? What's on?"

But he just sticks his phone near my face, and I grab it.

It's a text from a name I don't recognize.

**From Unknown**

> The Wolves won out. It's you and them for the tourney championship.

I look up at K. "We get our rematch!"

"But that's not even all of it. Read the next text," Special K says.

I read it and I almost drop the phone. "Wait, is this for real?"

Special K nods like some kind of bobblehead gone wild. He rubs his hands together like his master plan's finally coming together. "The *ultimate* revenge game."

We tell the rest of the team, and everyone is stunned.

J-Wu doesn't even believe it. "I gotta see it for myself."

It doesn't take long for J-Wu to get his wish.

During the pregame warm-up, we come out onto the court first. A few minutes later, here come the Wolves, and guess who's with them?

Yep, KO.

"Sup, fellas," he says, throwing us a head nod but strolling right past—like we're barely acquaintances.

Zay and I trade looks, and Special K won't stop nudging J-Wu. "Now what you got to say, J?" Special K keeps saying. "What I tell you?"

"Dang, we didn't beat them when *we* had KO and now they got him? For real, what we s'pose to do with that?" DJ complains.

"How can he even play? He shouldn't be eligible, right? He can't just walk onto their team in the middle of a tourney," Meeks chimes in.

Coach shakes his head. "The Wolves added him at the last minute. It's all perfectly within the rules."

Everyone groans. "That's trash. I can't believe he hooked up with those guys," DJ says.

But Coach isn't fazed. "What's going on with their team? That's none of our business. *Our* business is finishing what we didn't the last time we played them."

"Grudge match," I say.

Coach nods, then says those eight magic words: "One huddle, one hustle, one head, one heart!" And we shout them right back.

The first half we play them tough. Maybe they have a slight edge in talent, especially since adding KO, who's clearly the best player on either team—but we outmatch them in hustle and toughness. They're bigger than us, so you'd think they'd be the aggressor, that they'd be the physical team—but they're more finesse and skill than bruisers. Matter of fact, it's like those dudes are doing all they can to *not* be physical. It's a healthy dose of iso ball and three-point shooting.

Which means if they're hot, they can bury you in a hurry.

I'd seen it happen in most of their games, the other team doing its best to stay in the game, to chip away, but unable to mount a comeback against the barrage of threes.

The other thing about the Wolves? Their mouths pick right back up where they left off. They talk trash the *entire* game, with Trash-Talk King Dre taking the lead.

*This is gonna be hard to watch, this annihilation. Maybe y'all should close your eyes.*

*Yo, are those shoes orthopedics? My g-ma got them same shoes!*

But we don't back down and we don't lose our heads. We stay patient. We keep calm. We run our sets. We don't force anything. We push, we grind, we work.

As the second quarter ticks off its final seconds, we spring Meeks open for a wide-open corner three. He nails it, and we're up one. Our first lead of the whole game. Maybe there are only a few Sabre fans in the stands, but all four of them go wild, ha—and our whole bench is high-fiving and shouting *Let's goooo.*

But in a blink, the Wolves advance the ball upcourt. We scramble to stay in front of them, but we're a step slow, all the while Coach is yelling from the sideline, *Don't foul, do not foul!*

And we don't foul. But we do blow a switch at the top of the key that gives KO, with two seconds left, a wide-open look. The ball falls easy into the hoop.

As Wolves fans explode in cheers and his teammates congratulate him, KO doesn't react. He just turns and jogs back into the locker room. But the rest of the Wolves are more than enough hype to make up for KO's chill.

Their second-best player, a kid everybody calls Red, shouts across the gym, "Just so you know, there's plenty more where that came from. Y'all know you can't win."

I look at our guys, wondering who's gonna be the first to go back at the Wolves, but everyone's head is down.

And I can't explain it because even with KO's last-second heroics, we're still only down two. Except you wouldn't know it from the energy in our locker room.

"Why are we sitting here with long faces like we're getting our butts kicked?" Coach asks. "Guys, we're right where we wanna be. We're a couple of plays away from walking outta this gym winners."

Coach is right. "Let's go. We got this," I say as we head back out onto the floor. And even though we have a bit more pep, you can tell we don't really believe we can win.

By the end of the third quarter, we're down thirteen. Except it feels like thirty-three.

Halfway through the fourth, we're down twenty plus, and everyone in the gym knows it's over except Coach. "You wanna pull the starters, Coach?" I ask, and Kiara looks at me like *nooo.*

Coach turns to me, anger in his eyes. "Why would I do that?"

"I—I was just saying, so nobody gets hurt, maybe we should put our best players on the bench . . ."

But Coach isn't having it. "Nope. Our starters should be *embarrassed* by how awful they played. They're acting like we're playing at the park with their friends. Like this is a meaningless game. So they deserve to feel every second of this loss."

I nod. "I got you, Coach."

Coach swivels back courtside, and Kiara leans toward me. "You're both right. He should sit those guys. Save some of their juice for the next game. But also, they need to prove they've got heart to gut it out," she says.

"Yeah, you're right. They need to play with pride."

Coach calls time-out and lights into everyone for not playing hard anymore. For giving the game away. "I thought y'all were better than this. I thought y'all cared," he says.

And it works. Sparks a 14–2 run. And we're back to playing our style of ball. But the hole's too big to climb all the way out, and we take the hard L on the chin.

"Yo, good game, Sabres," KO says with a shrug. "Y'all almost made me break a sweat." And if I didn't know better, I'd almost think he was honestly complimenting us.

Except why would he?

The only thing KO's ever cared about is . . . KO.

But before we can reply, KO's dragged away by his new teammates, pulled into the center of the floor, where they pose for pics and celebrate.

And I'm not gonna lie to you. I hate every part of this feeling. It's not just the losing. It's not even that we lost to

KO. It's the way we lost. The way we stopped doing all the little things we normally do, like setting good screens and switching on defense. The way we didn't battle the second half the way we had the first.

The way we cracked under pressure.

"Championship teams don't turn it on and off. They're always on," Coach says on the flight home. "Y'all played like the moment was too big. Like you forgot who we are. We outwork everybody—that's our game. We want it more. That's why we win. But today, y'all played like you couldn't care less. That's not the Sabres I know."

And it's not the Sabres I know, either.

"We got some big tournaments ahead of us with some big-time competition. Now we're gonna find out what kind of team we really are. The kind that falls apart after a loss. Or the kind that rallies together and finds a way to win."

# 31

Turns out Terry's at the Philips Detention Center.

Until now, they wouldn't let anyone see him other than Aunt Tracy and his lawyer because he's *a violent threat*.

But then Munka and her friends make a video about Terry's arrest and what came before it—D's death, that Officer Truman didn't even get a suspension—and it goes viral.

And while the juvenile detention center doesn't release Terry right away, they do allow more visitors. Which is great because it means me, Dad, and Coach can finally make the thirty-minute drive. Inside Philips, the three of us move quietly through the building's security checks and metal detectors, before being led into an empty room, its cold concrete walls painted puke-your-guts-out green.

Ten minutes later, Terry shuffles in, escorted by a guard, who posts up a few feet away, scowling like he'd rather be anywhere but here.

"You okay, man?" is the first thing outta my mouth.

Terry nods, gliding his hand across the top of his wavy hair. "I'm good, bro. It's not so bad."

I shake my head. "Not so bad? Bro, you're basically in jail."

Terry smirks. "I'm basically a hero. Everybody hates twelve in here, so."

"Look, Terry, I know you're hurting bad, but I'm not sure you understand the gravity of this situation," Dad says.

"No, *you* don't get the gravity, man," Terry claps back. "Trust, I feel every bit of it."

Dad's mouth opens but he stops himself and leans back in his chair, his forehead creased.

Terry keeps going. "You ever watched your brother, your best friend, bleed out in the street? Huh? Have you? Because that's the *gravity* we talking, man."

Dad nods slowly. "None of this should have ever happened and I'm so sorry. I'm . . ." Dad pauses like the words are stuck in his throat. "I don't have the language to explain how much I feel for you. How much I hurt for you. D deserved better. You, your aunt, you all deserve better. No, I've never watched my brother die in the street. But I was your age when I lost my best friend." Dad turns away, like he's remembering something he'd rather not. "Bled out right in my arms. Shot over some stupid stuff."

"You never told me about that," I say to Dad.

Dad's eyes lock on mine and hold on to them tight like the tractor beams from *Space Explorers*. "Because I wanted better for you, Son. Because I hoped you'd never have to experience that pain. Because you shouldn't have to worry about dying. Because you should be running around with your friends, having fun, a long, happy life ahead of you. You shouldn't have to learn how to live with a giant hole in your heart. But now . . . now you know. And I'm so sorry I couldn't keep it away from you." Dad angles back toward Terry. "Both of you. The fact that we're having this conversation, that the world keeps robbing our young people of their joy, of their innocence, it makes me sick to my stomach."

"Dad . . ." I start, except I'm not sure what to say next.

But Dad's still wagging his head, his voice cracking. "I'm sorry I couldn't protect you from . . . from . . ."

Coach rests his hand on Dad's shoulder. "It's okay, brother," Coach says softly. "It's okay."

Dad buries his face in his hands, and I reach out but I'm afraid to touch him. Afraid that Dad will regret sharing his feelings with me. Afraid he'll pull away and go back to feeling nothing. Go back to being cold. Except now I know Dad *does* feel. Maybe he doesn't talk about them, but he has feelings, same as me. And it's wild, because all it took was sixty seconds of hard honesty for me to understand him a little more. One minute of *vulnerability*, one of Mom's favorite words, which means being real and open with the people you love, all the time knowing that if they wanted to, they could easily hurt you. It's strange—it's like we go through life without ever looking at each other, and everyone's just these blurry, faceless blobs. But one day you open your eyes all the way and *wham*, the world finally comes into perfect focus. Now you see the whole person. Suddenly, you see everything.

"You know, wasn't that long ago," Coach says, "I sat where you're sitting, Terry."

Terry's face twists like he's confused. "How you mean?"

"I mean I got into trouble. I made some tough choices that weren't wrong but also they weren't right. I made choices, all the while feeling like I didn't have a choice. And the things I did landed me here. In this same building. It's crazy, the walls are still the same ugly green."

Terry shakes his head. "You playing with me, right? No way you were here and still made it to the League."

Coach studies Terry carefully. "Why *no way*?"

Terry shrugs. "Because people who end up in places like this don't go nowhere else. Nowhere special, anyway. Don't matter how much talent you got. Nah, people like me? We never make it out."

Coach leans forward in his chair. "I believed that, too."

"Come on, Coach," Terry says, shaking his head. "This

the part where you give me the whole *hard work conquers all* speech, because no offense, but I've heard that before."

And Coach looks like he wants to blow his whistle, but instead, he says, "For real. I was like, *What's the point of doing things the so-called right way, if in the end I still end up nowhere?* I couldn't see past the end of my own nose. Not because I didn't want to. But because I didn't know anything *existed* beyond it."

Terry makes a face. "What's that even mean?"

Coach taps his nose. "It means the problem wasn't that I made the wrong choices. No, I made the only choices that were put in front of me. It's not that I was looking for trouble, or that I didn't respect authority, or that I was some clown who just didn't care. My family was hungry and we were poor, so I stole food from the grocery store. My shoes had more holes than Swiss cheese, so I went to the Shoe Barn and I walked out in some cheap sneakers I figured nobody was gonna buy, anyway. People love to talk about the plague of gang violence, and yeah, I saw it up close and personal. No question, it gets wild in these streets. But most of the dudes I knew who were in gangs? They joined up because they couldn't see any other way to survive. Because no one showed them anything different. No one told them they could be a doctor or a lawyer. Even if they had, there was no one there who could tell them *how* you became a doctor or lawyer. My older brother was in a gang. He joined because he was tired of getting robbed coming home from school. Because he wanted to protect our family. He joined so I didn't have to. But try explaining that to someone who grew up privileged and it's like trying to describe how water tastes to someone who's never taken a sip."

"Wow," me and Terry say at the same time.

"Coach, I didn't know you went through all of that," I add.

Coach nods. "I tell these stories and people think I'm glorifying being a thug or joining a gang or stealing, but the middle school I went to didn't have a working heater for two of the four years I went there, and you know how cold Milwaukee gets. Everybody in my class, including the teachers and principal, went to a school where some days it was warmer *outside*. Imagine that, living in the greatest country on earth, and not having heat at school. How are you gonna learn geometry with frostbite? But when people talk about kids in these underserved communities *choosing* to go down the wrong path, or making shortsighted decisions, they neglect to mention that when you're in the thick of it, when you actually live in these communities, you don't have a lot of options. You don't have *good* choices, only hard ones."

Terry wags his head. "That's how I felt with D. Like, if they can just come onto our court and shoot us with no consequences, how can we defend ourselves? What are we supposed to do when the people who are supposed to keep us safe are the ones hurting us? Why don't we get to feel protected? Everybody wanna see me go down for this, and okay, maybe there was another way to do it. Maybe so. But it didn't feel like there was another way that would actually make something happen."

Dad nods. "People who have *real* choices, actual resources, assume everyone else has the same opportunities. This country loves to talk about pulling yourself up by your bootstraps, but how you s'posed to do that without shoelaces?"

"Or without boots," Coach chimes.

"Ha," Dad says. "You ain't lying. But let the *haves* tell it and there's a pot of gold waiting for any person willing to *just work hard*. I work hard. I work three jobs. I ain't struck gold yet."

We all laugh, except it's the kind that doesn't last long, the kind of laughter that fades faster than it came.

"So how'd you make it out the hood, Coach?" Terry asks.

Coach shrugs. "I was lucky. Somebody gave me a second chance and told me that there wasn't gonna be a third one coming, so I either get right or get comfortable behind bars."

"So, just like that, you got yourself together?"

Coach shakes his head. "No. It wasn't easy. I had a lot of good people in my corner, though. People who saw the potential in me I couldn't see in myself. Kinda like . . . you. But you know why I really came back here after I stopped playing ball? Because I know what it feels like to not know what you're capable of. I know what it means to not know about all the opportunities that exist in this world. Because I remember the moment when I realized just how big the world is, and the moment I first saw I might have a future in it. Because I wanted to show kids like you, kids who are bright, tough, and occasionally funny . . . that there are more options, *better* options, to pick from. That if given the chance, our lives can go in so many incredible ways."

Terry turns away in his chair. "That's a good story, but I ain't some NBA legend in the making. Ain't nobody gonna care about me like that."

I reach out toward Terry, and the guard shoots me a look, like *back up*, so I do. "Terry, I care about you. Coach and Dad and everybody at school. In OS." I pause and look over at Coach. "I didn't even make the team. Not the way I wanted, and believe me, I thought I let everyone down. But . . . but as long as I try my hardest to do the right thing, I know I could never let any of you down. Not for real. Not for good. And now look at me, I'm using all my math nerdiness to help the Sabres."

Terry rubs his eyes, laughing a bit. "See, D told you all your nerdy ways would eventually pay off. But . . . what if it's too late for me?"

Dad waves his finger. "As long as you got breath in you, it's not too late."

Terry wipes his now-wet eyes. "If I ever get another chance, I'm not gonna screw it up. I promise y'all that. On everything."

"We know, Terry. We believe in you," Coach says. "That's why we're here."

"Ahem," I say, clearing my throat. "Can we tell him now? Because I'm not sure how much longer I can keep this inside."

Terry's eyebrows slide up. "Tell me what?"

Dad and Coach nod at me and I smile. "You're coming home, Terry."

"Wait, what?" Terry asks, his eyes bugging out so far, it's a miracle they stay in his head. "For real? When? How?"

"Now. With us," Coach says.

"We're taking you home."

"Okay, but how?"

"OS is how," I say. "The whole community's been on the phone, calling the mayor's office nonstop. It's all over social media and national news, too." My volume drops and, rolling my eyes, I add, "Plus, Munka, I guess."

"Munka what?" Terry asks.

"She got your story all over Twitter and IG," I say with a hard sigh. "I guess her having an iPhone for a best friend isn't all bad."

"Wow," Terry says, tears falling into his lap. "I can't believe y'all did that for me."

"Believe it, son," Dad says.

"And we'd do it again," Coach says. "But we better not have to."

And the four of us fall into a different kind of laughter.

The kind that comes when the knots in your stomach unravel and you're feeling relieved.

The kind when the Universe—like when a ref knows they made a mistake—gives you a makeup call. Is it better than not getting things wrong in the first place?

Nope.

But it's a start.

On the drive to OS, Coach and I tell Terry there's still a spot for him on the Sabres, if he's ever ready for it. "Not today," Terry says. "Not now. But never say never, right?"

We're not even out the elevator when Aunt Tracy comes racing outta their apartment, throwing both arms around Terry, even though he's taller than her, and lifting him off the ground in the biggest hug-slash-wrestling-move you've ever seen. "Don't you ever scare me like that again," she says softly. "You hear? Not ever again."

Terry nods. "I hear you," he says. "I promise."

# 32

Terry's home, and you'd think the world was made whole again, but there's still so much work to do. Yes, Terry being back in OS is the best off-the-court victory in a long time, but we've still gotta figure out a way to win on the court.

Luckily, Kiara and I are up to the task. Together, we watch more game tape than ever. We figure out that our full-court press isn't nearly as effective in the second half of games, which Coach says is due to poor conditioning. "We gotta get faster and stronger. We gotta play with high energy the entire game."

So we install new drills.

We lift more weights.

Practice harder than we've ever practiced.

And Coach's whistle, well, it blares less and less.

Plus, I unlock another key stat that was right under our noses the whole time: we're giving up the ninth-most points per game in the entire country, which is pretty awful defense . . . on the surface. But the truth is we average 14.5 more possessions than the next closest AAU team because we constantly push the pace, because we're always playing up-tempo.

And more possessions for us means more possessions for the other team, so of course we're gonna give up more points than other teams. But that's okay because we're also the fourth-*best* scoring offense in the nation, which means we are capitalizing on those extra possessions.

But that's also part of the reason we sometimes struggle in half-court offensive sets. We're used to running and swinging the ball for easy shots. But if we practice running a half-court offense, we'll be able to play both styles of ball—up-tempo and molasses, ha.

I tell Coach this, and he's all grinning. "Look at you," he says. "I told you you had it in you."

I smile back. "Sometimes you can't trust what you see on first glance, Coach. You gotta dig deeper. You gotta be *conscientious*."

We go on a wild run—winning a tourney in Charlotte, North Carolina.

We celebrate with a two-hour game of paintball.

Then we run through Minneapolis and celebrate that trophy with a pool party back at the rec down the street from OS. The whole neighborhood shows up, barbecuing and everything.

The point is: everywhere we go, we play with our heads on fire.

"We gotta be just as aggressive in the third and fourth as we are in the first and the second," I explain, rattling off a few more tendencies I've scouted, like the fact that we set 20 percent fewer screens in the second half of games. Or that our opponents' field goal percentage, while a stingy 38 percent in the first half of games, shoots up to 51 percent in the second halves.

We have a hiccup in Portland, matching up against the fourth-ranked fourteen-and-under team in the country.

"That can't happen," Kiara says as we watch Meeks lose his man in the paint, freeing our opponent to crash the offensive board and lay the ball in. "They're crushing us on the glass."

Coach calls time-out and encourages the guys to box out. "Let's go. I don't wanna see them grab another offensive rebound this whole game. Not one."

I stop Meeks before he can return to the court. "You good, man?" I ask him.

"Yeah, I'm good."

"I'm asking because the Meeks I know wouldn't be

getting killed in the paint like that. Not without a fight."

He shakes his head like I'm crazy. "Nobody's getting killed."

I hold up my stats clipboard for him to see. "This your man, right? And doesn't that say he's got fourteen points, five assists, *and* seven rebounds on you and we're not even out the third quarter. I don't know. I just figured you'd want to know."

Meeks doesn't reply. Not to me anyway. Not on the sideline.

He just goes out and shuts his man *down*.

"I don't know what you said to Meeks, but his man's not gonna score again. Not the way Meeks is smothering him," Kiara says halfway through the fourth.

Which is only mostly right.

When Coach subs in DJ for Meeks, Meeks's man gets fouled and hits one of two free throws. But then Meeks is back on him and it's curtains for their team. Meeks's matchup ends the game with fifteen points, six assists, and seven boards.

We cruise to a nineteen-point victory, and on the way back to the hotel, Meeks turns to me and gives me a head nod. "Thanks, bro."

I shake my head. "That was all you."

But Meeks waves me off. "We both know that's not true," he says.

# 33

## CLEVELAND, OHIO
### 24 DAYS TILL ORLANDO

Special K blocks eighteen shots and grabs sixty-four rebounds in two days and five games while Meeks goes on a scoring rampage, getting to the rack at will and forcing the opposing team into early foul trouble—we ride both guys all the way to the tourney championship game against the Miami City Cougars. The Cougars, a bunch of speedy, knockdown shooters, give us a good game—hitting what feels like a gazillion threes to keep them close. But up two with a minute thirty to go, Meeks weaves his way into the paint, drawing multiple defenders, before kicking the ball out to a wide-open J-Wu,

213

whose shot—after Coach's, D's, and Terry's—might be the best-looking stroke I've ever seen up close. The ball ripples through the net, putting us up by five and sealing the win.

"One huddle, one hustle, one head, one heart!" we sing in the locker room.

"We win together, we lose together," Coach reminds us.

Coach surprises us by getting us a tour inside the Field-House—where the Cleveland Cavaliers play. "Yo, Coach, you know where LeBron sat?" DJ asks when we walk into their locker room, all the players' names in plaques over their lockers, with leather chairs in front of each one.

"Nowhere you'd be sitting, bruh," Special K fires back before Coach can answer.

We take a million pics and videos at the Rock & Roll Hall of Fame—posing next to wax versions of Ray Charles and some original art drawn by a rap group called Public Enemy, who Coach told us made songs about fighting back against injustice, whether it was against the police or the government or whoever. *I don't advocate violence but we also can't do nothing. We have to use our voices. We have to use our power,* Coach said.

"So what do we do, Coach?" Meeks asks.

"Stay strapped, duh," Special K says, transforming his hand into a gun.

But Coach places his hand atop Special K's, like he's

helping him lower the weapon. Then Coach stands there a minute and says, "We can protest and form rallies. Make the government change the laws on how the cops police our communities. We can get involved with local politics and educate ourselves on the legal system."

"Like, learn *all the* laws?" DJ asks. "That's a lot."

Coach laughs. "No, not all the laws. But you know a lot of basketball rules, right?"

DJ nods. "Yeah."

"Because you understand that if you're gonna win a game, you gotta first know how to play it, yeah? It's the same with justice. You want it, you gotta learn it from the inside out, and then make it happen."

We annihilate the remaining competition in Cleveland.

"Yo, I can't wait for that revenge game against KO, though," J-Wu says, biting into a po' boy, a Cleveland thing that turns out to be Polish sausage in a bun stacked with French fries and coleslaw. I've had worse.

"Tell me about it," Zay says, stealing a fry from my tray. "At the science center, I couldn't even enjoy that nature video because it kept talking about wolves. I used to love wolves, but those fools stole that from me, too."

I try to keep everybody's heads right, though. "It's not about KO. We can't make it personal. That's how we lose."

"Honestly, it felt like KO wasn't even there with those guys," Meeks says.

J-Wu frowns. "What you mean? Dude had twentysome-thing points, and he sat the entire fourth quarter."

"I don't mean like that. He balled out because KO always balls out. I just mean it felt like he wasn't really a part of their team. Like, he was by himself."

Zay shrugs. "That just sounds like classic KO to me."

"No, I know what you mean, Meeks," I say, scooping up a spoonful of coleslaw. "He was definitely on some other stuff that day."

Zay laughs. "Like I said, classic KO."

"Next time we see them, we're gonna go right at them. Make them feel us," J-Wu says.

"My man," Zay says, exchanging daps. "I can't wait till that game."

Waiting at the gate for our plane to board, we teach Coach the latest dance, and not gonna lie, he kinda kills us—*yeah, you can post that*, he says triumphantly, pointing at Kiara, who recorded the whole thing on her phone for the social media account she created for the team.

*The more people that know about us, the better chance for our guys to get offered scholarships*, she said. Which is something we talk about all the time—guys earning scholarships on the court, but Coach never lets us go too far. *I want you all to play at the next level, but most importantly, no matter what happens on these courts, I want all of you to go to school at the next level and earn a college degree.*

"Why does he do it?" I ask Kiara on the plane ride back home.

"Why does *who* do *what*?"

"Your dad," I say, nodding toward Coach James, who's laughing with Johnny and Zay about something in the row ahead of us. "Why does he do *all this*? With *us*? He could be coaching some college team or be an assistant in the NBA. He could open a restaurant or a car wash or something. Anything but come back here to Milwaukee. To Racine."

And she doesn't answer for a minute, so I wonder if she's heard me, but then she tilts her head in this way she does when she's really thinking something through. And finally, she says, "Because he's from OS, too. Because he was you. Because he *is* you."

# 34

Even with all the travel and touring and excitement, even after experiencing stuff we couldn't have even dreamed of before, we're still not prepared for the biggest turnaround of all time.

We get word that there's been a huge break in Dante's case—there's an eyewitness who's come forward. Someone who actually saw Officer Truman shoot D. Someone willing to go on record *against* the police, even though it could mean retaliation or intimidation.

When a news reporter asks why come forward now—so many weeks later—the woman, a thirtysomething single mom whose fiancé died in military service, says her only regret is not coming forward sooner. "It doesn't matter how much time's passed," she says, standing bravely in front of the camera. "Right is right, and there's no expiration date on justice."

Her testimony alone is enough to force the prosecutor to reopen the investigation. Except the good news doesn't stop there—because *another* eyewitness pops up, an older OS resident with dementia—which Dad says means the old man forgets things a lot—who says he was recording his favorite bird perched outside his window when he heard shouting down in the courtyard. Without even thinking, he pointed his camera phone down at D, only moments before the shots were fired. He'd forgotten he even had the footage until his granddaughter found it on his phone and took it down to the police station—but not before she uploaded it on social media. The video is spreading faster than fire.

"What's it mean?" Tasha asks across the dinner table.

"It means they're finally gonna lock up the cop who shot Dante," Munka explains.

"It means they know they got it wrong the first time. Means maybe we can finally get justice for D," I add.

"Maybe," Big Mama says. "Hopefully."

"You still don't think it's gonna happen? How could they not with all this evidence?" I ask her.

"I think you shouldn't get your hopes too high," Big Mama warns. "They like to do stuff like this. Make us believe just for a moment that maybe justice is actually possible, before reminding us that, even if it is, it's nearly improbable."

Lying in bed, I think about that all night—*justice is possible but improbable.*

And then, with the perfect timing only the Universe can pull off, I get:

**From Terry**

> Cool if we talk?

I text Coach, *Terry wants to talk,* and Coach hits me back right away.

> Take all the time you need. Let me know if I can do anything to help.

We meet at the one place that a month ago I wasn't sure I'd ever be able to set foot on.

Paradise Court. There are still a few blown-out candles, and stuffed animals, and homemade cards surrounding a large photo of D, arranged along the wire fence.

We don't walk across the court, though. We walk around it, taking our time, like we're waiting for something to happen. We don't talk for a while, and then Terry finally says, as we're walking outta OS, "Heard you guys been playing lights out."

I smile. "We're doing okay. Wish you were with us," I say, immediately wishing I could take back those last words. *Wish you were with us.*

Terry must wish I could take them back, too, because he

goes quiet again—and the only thing I hear is my own stupid heart beating loudly and the Don't Walk sign buzzing right above our heads, hanging from the corner traffic pole, where we wait to cross.

"It's good they're reopening the case," I say, breaking the silence as we make it across, pausing in front of the bus stop, the bus only a block away, waiting for its own light to turn green.

Terry frowns. "Hopefully, they get it right this time . . ." His voice trails off.

At first, I think it's because he's emotional, but then I follow his eyes and I see it, too.

The black SUV.

The older dudes Terry was hanging with.

The truck slows down to a crawl on the street next to us and honks, but Terry barely waves back.

"What, you not kicking it with those guys anymore?"

Terry shakes his head. "Like I said the day y'all picked me up. I'm not screwing up again."

"Good," I say as we board the bus. "Because I didn't wanna have to kick your butt."

Terry cracks up like it's the funniest thing he's ever heard—which, if you ask me, is waaay too much.

Inside Coach's office it happens so fast, even though on the ride to the Bray, Terry's all, *But what if Coach changed his mind?*

"He didn't," I assure him. "He wouldn't. But even if he did, basketball's not the only way on the team. The Tony Washington Sports Probability Firm is always on the lookout for fresh new talent."

And we both crack up this time, Terry shaking his head. "Seriously, how long you been waiting to say that?"

In the end, I don't get to welcome Terry to the firm because Coach takes him back with open arms.

"Far as I'm concerned, you were never *not* a part of our Sabre family," Coach tells him. "But you're behind, so don't be upset when I work you hard."

Terry nods, smiles for maybe the first time in forever. "I wouldn't expect anything less, Coach." And then, "I'm ready to put the time in. Whatever it takes, I'm ready."

"Born ready," I add, because you don't even have to ask—I'm always down to insert the corny.

# 4TH QUARTER

## 35

Our team was already on a roll—over the last two weeks, we moved from number nineteen to number twelve—but after adding Terry and his shooting stroke to our rotation, we breeze through the competition. Seriously, every time Terry hoists a jumper from distance, the whole bench explodes in celebration even before the shot falls. It's hard to explain, but just having Terry around, even if he wasn't Mr. Automatic, it's like we've unlocked a cheat code for fun. Everybody's spirits are up a thousand since he joined the squad.

Plus, the latest poll has us jumping five spots—yep,

you're looking at the number-seven-ranked team in the entire country. Now all we had to do was stay the course and Orlando was almost a lock . . . not that it was gonna be easy. After all, the higher your ranking, the harder your opponents try to take you down.

"I'm glad you changed your mind," I tell Terry enough times that I lose count.

But he doesn't get sick of the compliment. He just grins and nods *me too*.

The timing's perfect, too—Terry becoming a Sabre right before we start our hometown tourney. It's awesome traveling all over the country, seeing landmarks and trying new food, bonding with the team on the road—but it's kinda nice to kick it in our hometown, too. Plus, it means everyone's family and friends can come to our games.

But another reason it's cool to have Terry sharpshooting us to victory?

Because you never wanna lose to a team from your *same* city in your *own* city, not with bragging rights up for grabs, not when you know you're gonna see those dudes all the time, at the grocery store, at the movies, and back at school once summer vacation's over.

"But playing at home also means more distractions," Coach warns after an especially exhausting practice. "So let's make sure we keep the same focus we've had on the road, yeah?"

"Yes, sir," the team chirps back.

"All right, good work today. Zay, break us down," Coach says. And we all squeeze into a tight huddle, everyone putting one hand in the middle.

"Hustle hard on three," Zay barks. "One, two, three—"

"Hustle hard!" the whole team echoes.

I'm gathering my bag to review some film with Coach and Kiara, when Special K starts shouting and waving his phone in the air.

"What are you so hype about?" I ask.

"Guess who's officially invited to Orlando?" Special K asks, smiling.

And you know that saying: *You got the whole squad laughing?*

Ha, I'll do you one better: we got the whole squad celebrating.

Everybody goes wild, even Coach is mad hype, all of us hugging and jumping up and down like we won the lottery. But we kinda did, in a way . . .

Because the odds of us making it to Orlando, after all that's happened?

Slim.

But here we are, on our way.

Florida, here we come.

"Just because we're invited to Orlando doesn't mean we stop working hard," Coach says after a particularly grueling practice. "If anything, we work harder. Because I don't know about y'all but I'm not happy just to be at the tournament. I'm trying to come home with some serious hardware. What y'all think?"

"Yes, Coach," we all shout in unison.

"This is only the beginning," DJ chimes.

Meeks smiles. "We didn't come this far to fall apart at the end, feel me?"

"Championship or bust," I add.

"Hey, guys," J-Wu interrupts frantically. "Guys, check this out," he says, holding up his phone like it's some kind of treasure map.

"Yo, what's up, bro?" Zay asks.

J-Wu smiles. "Looks like there's gonna be a few familiar faces joining us in Orlando . . ."

Zay takes J-Wu's phone, scrolls down. "Ha, looks like we get the chance to redeem ourselves."

But Special K's shaking his head like *nope*. "Bump all that redemption talk. I'm not interested. We 'bout to prove who the better team really is. Bring on the Wolves. We're ready."


Dad's car is parked in Big Mama's driveway, which is weird because he should be at work.

My mind immediately starts flipping through worst-case scenarios—what if Dad lost one of his jobs? What then?

Except inside I hear laughter coming from the kitchen.

My brain flops the other way. *What if Mom's back?*

"What's going on in here?" I ask, racing around the corner. And everybody's there: Dad, Munka, Tasha, and Big Mama. Well, almost everybody.

My face drops a bit, and Dad shakes his head. "Why you looking like somebody just told you you were ugly?"

I shrug. "No reason. I guess I just thought that maybe Mo—"

Tasha leaps into my arms. "We're going to Disney World! We're gonna see Princess Jasmine!"

"Wait, what?"

Dad nods, hands me his phone, and I can't believe it. "You bought plane tickets?"

Dad grins. "You know we can't miss the big rematch."

"But how can we afford this?"

"What's the point of working so hard if you can't support the people you love?" Dad asks. "As long as you're under our roof, you never have to worry about money, Tone. That's me and your mom's thing. And we always got you, right?"

I nod. "Right," I say. "You coming, too?" I ask Big Mama.

She laughs. "Boy, you think I'm passing up a chance to ride the Tower of Terror?"

## ORLANDO, FLORIDA

This is the best hotel room I've ever been in.

"Is this how rich people's houses are?" I ask, examining a collection of small bottles and soaps next to the giant bathroom sink. "With the toilet and shower in a room by themselves and the sink on the outside?"

But Terry doesn't hear me. He's too busy messing around behind me. "Dude, you see the size of this TV?" Terry exclaims, moving it back and forth from the wall. "And it's adjustable. Nothing worse than a TV sitting on some funky angle. That's how you wake up with a jacked-up neck."

I pop open the little lotion bottle. "Wow. This actually smells good."

Terry laughs. "You really in here sniffing lotion, bruh?"

I shrug. "I figured hotel lotion was trash. But this smell . . ." I pause to read the label. *Cedarwood infused with lavender notes.* "It's . . . relaxing."

Terry shakes his head. "It's all yours, man. I gotta use special lotion anyway. Anything else dries out my skin. Can't be out on the court with ashy ankles. Girls ain't tryna talk to you when your skin looks like you been rolling in cake flour."

I crack up. "You funny. Where you get stuff from, Terry?"

"I pay attention, bruh," Terry explains, tapping his finger on his brain. "People think I'm not watching, not listening, but I am. All the time. And I notice things. Patterns. The way stuff really works. Then I just file it away until I need it, you know?"

I nod even though I'm not 100 percent sure I get it—what I do get is that Terry's the kinda dude everybody sleeps on like *he's weird*, and then, like, ten years later, you find out, no, he's just a low-key genius or whatever. I got a cousin like that in Ohio. Now he's building rockets for NASA.

Terry throws his bag onto the bed closest to the door. "I gotta take this bed. Cool?" But I don't even answer before Terry's explaining why. "There's a crazy draft coming from the window, and I can't sleep with cool air hitting me like that. I'll wake up sick."

My eyebrows slide up, and I cackle. "Dude, *what*?"

But he's mad serious. "Why you think I always sleep with socks on, bruh?" Terry asks, as if it's scientific fact that sock-less sleep is a surefire way to catch the flu. Apparently, that's

231

also why Terry *has* to wear at least a T-shirt. "No sleeping in tanks or bare-chested, can't even do it, bruh. Unless you tryna see me all snot-nosed and red-eyed come morning."

I throw up my hands to stop him. "I don't even need to know all that," I say, smiling. "Whatever you need, man. I'll sleep wherever. You the one playing tomorrow. I'm just chilling on the bench. We need you at your best."

Terry nods. "Appreciate you, bruh. If D was here, he'd make us shoot for it."

I laugh. "Dang, you right."

"Nobody loved competition more than my brother. Nobody," Terry says, balling up his chicken sandwich wrapper and lobbing it toward the trash can across the room. It bounces off the wall and drops in, Terry smiling hard. "See? Man, I even shoot trash crazy smooth, haha."

"Nah, man, you ain't call glass, so that ain't count, sorry."

Terry laughs, waves me off. "Man, you crazy. I called it. You just ain't hear. It was under my breath."

I shake my head. "Sorry, you gotta take the window," I say, hopping onto "Terry's" bed.

And then Terry's jumping on the bed with me and now we're wrestling, trying to push each other on the floor, and we're cracking up, shouting at each other to give up, until two loud bangs ring out from the other side of the wall. From the room next door.

"Settle down in there, unless y'all wanna sleep on the bus," Coach shouts from his room. Except you can tell he's not really mad, and after a minute, Terry whispers, "Not Coach yelling through *whole walls* for us to be quiet . . ."

And we try to hold our laughs in, but it only makes us laugh harder.


After team dinner, we all crowd into J-Wu's room and go at it on his PS5 until Ms. Carter comes looking for Zay and tells him it's bedtime.

"But, Mama, I'm in here killing these boys with Kyrie. Just let me finish this . . ."

But Ms. Carter makes her *I'm not playing* face, and then Zay's passing the controller to DJ and stretching his arms in a pretend yawn. "Yo, I *am* kinda tired, though," he says. "I'mma hit the bed, give somebody else a chance to win."

"Sweeet dreeeams, Zay," the whole team sings as Zay slides into the hallway with his mom.

I nod and dap everybody. "I'm out, too. Gonna watch some more film."

"Love to see it, Coach Tone," Special K says, tapping my fist with his own.

Sitting at the desk, I get so lost watching the game tape, scouting the other team for the millionth time, that I don't even realize Terry's turned off most the lights. That he's already catching z's.

I close the laptop, brush my teeth, and climb into my bed.

"Hey, Tone," Terry mumbles, his voice raspy with sleep.

"Sup?" I ask. I can barely make out his body in the dark.

"That thing you said earlier? About the team needing me at my best?"

I nod even though he probably can't see me. "What about it?"

"It's you, too," Terry says softly. "We gonna win, we need you at your best, too."

And I don't know what to say. All I know is I *feel* a lot right now.

I feel seen.

I feel heard.

I feel like I . . . matter.

"Thank you," I say finally. But I'm too late, Terry's already back to purring, lost in some dream hopefully.

Honestly, I prefer the window. It's like being home in my own bed. Going to bed with the moon on my face, waking with the sun in its place.

Except I don't hear the gravel crunching tonight. I don't hear the ball bouncing off the pavement, off the backboard. D's quiet tonight.

Tonight, downtown Orlando dominates the skyline. The window glass thick enough to block out most of the noise, but the loudest sounds still slip through—

The blare of a car horn.

The whir of a siren.

The low thump of a party happening somewhere, people dancing, singing, having a good time. And it's like if you pay attention, if you listen like Terry said, you get to see and hear parts of the world other people miss. And I don't wanna miss not one thing. No, I wanna soak in every drop of every moment. I wanna drink it all in, like the world's a glass of water, just waiting for you to throw it back and gulp.

# 37

So, Orlando is *hot*.

You can actually see the air, that's how thick it is.

The tourney's held in a local college arena, and it's one of the nicest courts we've been on, except we're all soaked in sweat before we even make it inside the gym.

We start slow, tired from travel and heat, but we quickly get our legs under us and then we're off to the races. We run through our first two games like the other teams are made of single-ply toilet paper—it's almost too easy.

After we crush the San Diego Destroyers, our last matchup of the day, by twenty-six points, we decide to celebrate at the Pizza Piggy, home to the best double-stuffed crust I've ever had. The manager recognizes us, tells us he was born and raised in Milwaukee, that he's been following us online and that we're doing our city proud. We all cheer when he tells us pizza, breadsticks, and drinks are on the house.

"Can't believe I'm saying this, but we need more competition. Harder games," J-Wu says, dipping a stick in a cup of marinara. "We gotta be battle-tested before we play the Wolves again."

Meeks shrugs, pours himself more water. "We *are* tested. We're not beating down teams because we're more talented. We're winning because we've upped our game. We're focused."

Zay nods. "No one plays harder than us."

"That's cuz no one's coached harder than us," J-Wu says, laughing. "We're up five hundred points and Coach is still yelling, *Get back on D, stop playing lazy.*"

"Because Coach knows that we can't afford any letup. Not against the top teams. Definitely not against the Wolves," I say.

"We all know where we went wrong last time," DJ says, chewing on a wedge of stuffed crust. "We played tight that second half. We were playing *not to lose* instead of playing to win."

Terry slurps his soda. "Yeah, and we got exposed."

"Yeah, well," Special K says, winking. "This time we're gonna do the exposing. Watch."

I shake my head. "You guys are assuming we win our

next three games and that the Wolves win out, too. Either of us loses and you can kiss the rematch goodbye."

Zay taps his phone screen. "You see the rest of our bracket? If we lose any of those games, we don't deserve another crack at the Wolves."

So, naturally, the very next day we find ourselves in the toughest game we've had in weeks.

The Chicago Fire is that rare combination of size and skill. They've got the bodies to bully you in the paint *and* the shooters dancing around the perimeter to punish you for double-teaming.

Special K's having a rough game, and after having three of his layup attempts swatted into the stands, he's rushing his shot. Coach James calls time-out with us down four with only three minutes left in the game. The guys huddle around our bench. "Tell him what you told me," Coach says, turning to me.

"Special K, you're dipping your left shoulder. That's how he knows where you're going with the ball."

Special K wags his head. "My bad. I'll clean it up."

"No," I say. "Dip again, but next time, spin back to your other hand."

Coach James nods. "How are we on the glass, Tone?"

I look at my stat sheet. "We're down six rebounds."

Coach claps his hands. "Box out. Box out. Box out. We rebound as a team."

And we do rebound. The next time Special K gets the ball on the low block, he dips his shoulder like he's been doing all game, and his defender, who can probably *taste* the block coming, cheats to the baseline. Except this time, Special K pivots right toward the center of the paint and shoots a soft hook that glides through the nylon.

Behind us, in the stands, Munka, Big Mama, and Ms. Carter are so hype, I wouldn't be surprised if they laced up and ran on court.

Over the final two minutes, we play tenacious defense and fight for every board, collecting two timely offensive rebounds that we convert into easy putbacks. We close the game out on an 8–0 run.

"That's how you play with composure," Coach says, smiling. "Good teams are gonna make a few runs against us, but we gotta keep our heads. Stick to our game."

J-Wu rubs his hands together. "Bring on the Wolves," he says.

And I wait for Coach to lecture us about overconfidence, but instead he nods. "Bring on the Wolves," Coach agrees. "We're ready."

Coach calls an emergency team meeting down in the hotel lobby, and we're all thinking, *Uh-oh, what's going on?*

But when we get there Coach is dressed . . . funny.

"Coach, why you in palm-tree Bermuda shorts, man?" Special K chimes.

"And those toes," Special K chimes.

Coach looks down at his flip-flopped toes and frowns. "What's wrong with my toes?"

Special K stops laughing. "Nothing, Coach. They're lovely."

And we all bust out laughing again.

Coach shakes his head. "The reason I called this meeting

is because I wanted to let you know that today's practice is . . . canceled!"

"Wait, for real?" DJ asks.

"For real," Coach confirms. "Today, the only thing I want us to focus on is having fun."

"But what about the Wolves tomorrow?" J-Wu asks. "Shouldn't we be, like, preparing?"

Coach smiles. "We are preparing. We've been grinding for weeks. We've pushed ourselves, and we've grown. But there's another part to the game that I don't want us to forget."

"What's that, Coach?" Zay asks.

"We're not just a team when we're on the court," Coach says. "The best teams I've ever been a part of? We were tight off the court, too. Now I know most of you guys are friends, but I want everybody on this team to look out for each other, no matter what, no matter where. One huddle, one hustle, one head, one heart . . . Now let's go to Disney World!"

Turns out Disney World is huge.

"So, what should we do first?" Coach asks.

Big Mama raises her hand like we're in school. "The Tower of Terror."

In the end, we do almost everything—and Coach is right, team bonding is just as important as how we perform on the court.

Zay and his mom are all about the big rides, while Coach, Kiara, and Mrs. James are more interested in the food. "There's so many international flavors," Mrs. James says, like she's on one of those cooking shows.

J-Wu, Terry, and DJ are all about the carnival games, and we spend a full hour shooting at these super-firm hoops, trying to win a giant purple stuffed panda. Kiara wins it and hands it to me and Coach is all clearing his throat hard, but Mrs. James makes me and Kiara take a picture together. "Make sure you keep the panda in the middle," Coach directs.

Probably the biggest surprise of the day is Special K, who refuses to get on a single ride. "Bro, me and heights don't mix well, okay," he tells me when I try convincing him to at least try one.

And Munka comes leaping to his rescue. "Don't give him a hard time. It's hard admitting your fears," she says.

And me and Dad exchange looks like, *oh boy*.

Big Mama wasn't wrong about the Tower of Terror— it's wild. You're with a bunch of people sitting in this dark room, and then, all of a sudden, it feels like you're dropping a million miles per hour. Like, your stomach flies up into your throat.

Tasha's just tall enough but Dad's still all, "You sure you're not scared?"

But then the ride starts and it's Dad who's screaming his butt off. "It's too fast! Get me off!"

Our whole family is cracking up, and Tasha takes Dad's hand and says, "It's okay, Daddy. I'm here. I won't let anything bad happen to you."

I can't lie, though. As much fun as we have as a family, as a team, I miss Mom. I can't stop thinking about how much she'd love this.

"I thought she'd be up for it," Dad tells us while we're standing in line for another ride. "But she just needs a bit more time."

We FaceTime her on the ride back to the hotel, and she's smiling, asking us to tell her all about it. "I'm so sorry I can't be there," she says, her eyes tearing up. "I promise I'll make it up to you guys."

I shake my head. "You don't have anything to make up for," I tell her. "We're just happy you're getting rest, Mom."

Munka nods, wipes her own eyes. "Don't worry, Mom, I'm keeping everybody in line."

Mom laughs. "Now I know that's *not* true. Especially if your grandma's there."

"Heyyy! I heard that!" Big Mama says, cracking up, and we turn the phone toward her so Mom can see her. "Hey, Maggie, you're looking good, baby."

"Thanks, Big Mama," Mom says. "I gotta go to the next session now, but I'll talk to you guys later, yeah?"

We all crowd into the video and say our goodbyes.

Big Mama says sometimes people's brains won't let them be the happy people they are inside. That the place where

Mom is has people who *specialize* in helping people be happy again.

"Like therapy?" Tasha asks.

"What you know about therapy?" Big Mama shoots back.

Tasha shrugs. "Just that the doctor woman on TV said we all need it."

Big Mama nods. "Well, the doctor's not wrong."

"Everybody needs help sometimes," Dad says.

And I get it, but it's still hard, to see someone you love struggling. To be so far apart and not know when you'll see them again. All I know is, I love Mom, we all do, and I want her to be as happy as she makes us.

We end the day at the ocean.

And I've been to beaches. I've seen lakes and a couple of ponds. But this? This is next-level. "Whoaaaa" is all I can say as we march toward the water.

"Dude, it sounds like the ocean's roaring," Zay says.

Tasha grabs Terry's hand and makes him run toward the waves to get her feet wet; Dad and Big Mama trail after them, Big Mama calling after Tasha that she needs to put on more sunscreen—and Tasha calling back over her little shoulder, "Dad says Black people don't burn."

Some of the team fling a Frisbee back and forth across the sand, but a few of us stand shoulder to shoulder along the shore, the water sloshing bits of shell and seaweed between our toes.

We stand there for a long time without saying a word. Just watching the waves jump over each other. It's wild—no matter how hard I squint, I can't see where the water ends. It just keeps going and going as far as my eyes can see, until, eventually, it's hard to know what's ocean and what's sky.

And I make a promise to myself: one day I'm gonna bring my whole family back here. We're gonna stand right here on the edge of the whole world, on this same sand on the same beach, and stare out at these same waves.

"Can you believe this even exists?" Special K asks. "Like, I've seen movies and pictures, but it's like, who knew all this stuff was a thing?"

"Who knew Milwaukee wasn't the center of the world?" DJ says. "I thought I wanted to play ball at Marquette, but now I kinda wanna play outta state."

I nod. "Why is that a bad thing?"

DJ shrugs. "I don't wanna leave everybody behind. Leave everything I know behind."

Meeks squeezes DJ's shoulder. "You're not. You're just setting yourself up for your best possible future. Nothing wrong with that."

J-Wu skips a stone across the waves. "Besides, it's like with Coach. You go do your thing, and you can always come home."

Tasha asks me to tuck her in.

Except there weren't enough rooms at our team hotel,

so my family's in a hotel a few blocks away. Coach has the team bus drop us off first, and I fist-bump Zay, tell him I'll catch up with him later.

Tasha makes me read three stories to her before she's ready to sleep. I kiss her forehead.

"You're gonna be great tomorrow," she says.

I smile down at her. "Thanks, Tasha."

But she's already drifting off to dreamland.

Munka's locked herself in the bathroom, talking on her phone, and Big Mama's picking at a salad she bought from the hotel restaurant. Dad's chilling on the sofa, watching an NBA classic game on ESPN.

"Night, Dad," I say.

"Heading back to the team?"

I nod.

"I'll walk you down," he says.

"You don't have to do that," I say, but he's already following me to the door.

The elevator ride down's quiet until an older woman with a Chihuahua climbs in on the third floor. The little dog doesn't stop yelping, no matter how many times she shushes it.

"You nervous about tomorrow?" Dad asks as we push through the hotel doors out onto the sidewalk.

I shake my head, but then I tell the whole truth. "A little. But I'm not really that involved, I'm just the statistician."

Dad clutches both of my shoulders. "Tone, don't ever say you're *just* anything. You hear me? You *are* involved. The team counts on you. Coach counts on you. You know how many times he's told me how proud of you he is? How the team wouldn't be where it is without you?"

My face twists in surprise. "Coach said that?"

"He did." Dad sighs. "Honestly, it made me think about how often I tell you I'm proud of you . . ."

"It's cool, Dad. I know you are, even if you don't say it."

"I'm glad you know. But I should say it. You deserve to hear it from me. Maybe I take for granted that you and your sisters are so smart and stay outta trouble. Maybe I just assume you know how much I appreciate how hard you work at school and now with this team. I see how much it means to you. And that makes it matter to me, too. Because the thing is, I *am* proud of you, Tone. I'm so very proud. And it has zero to do with whether or not you dribble the ball on the court or you take notes on the sideline."

I'm not gonna lie. My eyes maybe get wet, but you know, it's probably because I got a bit of that red onion on my fingers from Big Mama's salad. Or maybe I'm allergic to that yelping Chihuahua. I can't really say *why* my eyes are watering. Only that I don't remember feeling like this before. It's not like he never tells me, *Good job.* It's not like he doesn't believe in me. I know he does. But hearing those words from his own lips, knowing from Big Mama that my grandpa almost never told anyone he loved them, least of all his only son, my dad—

I guess it makes me feel . . . proud back.

"I love you, Dad."

"I know you do. I feel it right here," Dad says, jabbing his chest with his long finger. "I love you, Tone."

And we stand there on the sidewalk, traffic whizzing by, not knowing what else to say . . . so I just double down on the awkward and hug him.

I'm waiting for the elevator when someone calls my name.

It's Kiara. "Come on," she says, waving me down the hallway toward the pool.

"I don't have trunks," I say.

She laughs. Points to her neon green tank and black running shorts. "Does it look like I'm going swimming?"

"Where you taking me?" I ask, following her down the hallway.

"You'll see. Don't you like surprises?"

I shrug. "Honestly, I don't know," I say. "Most of the surprises in my life haven't been all that great."

"Well, your luck's about to change," she says, pushing through a door marked *Banquet Hall A*.

It's one of the biggest, fanciest rooms I've ever seen, outside of a stadium or arena. There are lots of round tables with white linen tablecloths and big, heavy-looking chandeliers hanging from the ceiling, their clear crystals catching and reflecting every trace of light.

But I don't even get to fully process everything because the door we just came in—it opens again and in comes the rest of the team.

"Yo, why Coach tell us to come down here? We having an awards show, ain't we? He about to crown me team MVP, right?" Special K says, laughing hard at his own joke.

But then a door at the far end of the room pops open and a hotel worker enters pulling a huge trolley behind him. His trolley stacked with probably fifteen, twenty cardboard boxes. Then another hotel employee comes behind him with another trolley of boxes. And then two more with two more trolleys.

Until there are about eighty stacked boxes in front of us.

"What is this?" I ask Kiara.

But Kiara only smiles.

The door opens one last time, and in walks Coach.

"What's up, Coach? Why all the boxes? You moving to Orlando or something?" Meeks asks.

"They're for you," Coach says.

"Say what?" DJ shoots back.

Coach smiles. "Your names are on them. What are you waiting for? Open them up."

Except at first no one moves, because we're all still like, *Wait, what—*

So of course, we get the last sound in the world we ever wanna hear: *Shroot! Shroot!*

Yep, that blasted whistle.

But it does the job because next thing I know everyone's racing over to the boxes, calling out the names on the boxes until everyone has their stack.

"Open them up," Coach says, laughing.

And we can hardly believe our eyes.

"Ohmigod, dude, is this real?" DJ screams.

Zay's nodding like he might pass out. "Yo, I don't even know. I'm thinking *not*."

I open my first box, and inside I find: Nike basketball shoes in our electric-blue-and-white team colors *with* our team names on the back of the heels. "Get outta here!" I say.

"This is crazy, y'all," Special K keeps saying as we all keep unboxing.

There are matching headbands, wristbands, sleeves, long socks, short socks, and tanks.

There are custom white home jerseys with electric-blue trim and black away jerseys with electric-blue-and-white trim that say *Oasis Springs* across the chest.

"These are sick," Meeks says, slipping the black over his T-shirt and taking a selfie.

There are four pairs of shoes for each of us—black, white, blue, and these crazy glow-in-the-dark joints that look wild at night. Plus, there are duffel bags and backpacks, too.

"Thank you so much, Coach," everyone keeps saying.

And Coach nods. "You all deserve this and more," he says. "This is only the beginning. We're just getting started."

"You knew about this?" I ask Kiara.

"Maybe," she says, winking.

"Now we keeping secrets, huh?" I tease.

"Man, we doing whatever needs done," she says, grinning, motioning to all my new gear stacked in a pile that's not much shorter than me. "So which thing's your favorite?"

"Hmm," I say, like I'm thinking hard, but I already know. It's the one thing still in the box.

An all-black Nike swoosh drawstring bag, the same one D wore.

I slip it onto my shoulders, and it feels right.

And I know everything Coach said is true.

This is barely the beginning.

Because to reach our goals, not just now, but the future— man, we've got a long way to go yet. We've barely scratched the surface of what we can do when we believe in ourselves. When we believe in each other.

But we're getting there.

We're gonna get there.

And when we do, when we finally put it altogether, man, world, you better watch out, is all I'm saying. You better watch all the way out.


Before dragging my new haul up to the room, I find Coach and hug him.

"I don't know what to say except thank you. Feels like there's probably a better way to tell you. Words I don't have but . . ."

But Coach is patting my back and saying, "No better words than those right there."

I nod and start for the door before stopping, pivoting back like a move in the post. "Hey, Coach?"

"Sup?"

"You think we could talk to one of your old college coaches?"

"Sure. You mean about trying to get a scholarship?"

I shake my head. "No, I was thinking we could talk about what it takes to become a professional statistician. You know, like in the League."

Coach smiles. "Oh, we can definitely do that. I'm going to text a few people right now."

"Cool," I say, smiling back. Because sometimes you surprise yourself.

"Wow, bro," Special K chimes, shaking his head. "Did you really just ask to talk to other math nerds about how to be more mathematically nerdy?"

# 39

It's not that I *don't* sleep. More like I sleep in *spurts*.

Like when you get hot and go on a 12–0 run, but then the other team heats up and put up ten unanswered. All night it's like me and Team No Sleep are playing one-on-one. And when I do manage to catch a few z's, guess what animal shows up in my dreams—or should I say nightmares?

Yep, a whole wolf pack.

"Yo, you good, bruh?" Terry says from the other bed, lying on his side with his back to me. "You get any sleep?"

I sit up, look out the window, the sun already halfway up the sky. "Yeah," I say. "I got enough."

It's a forty-five-minute ride to the arena.

And I don't know if it's because we're all tired or what, but mostly, for the first time ever, the bus is kinda quiet. I close my eyes, but I don't sleep. I just imagine the plays Coach and I have been studying, the plays the guys have been practicing. I think about battling KO again and how it feels weird to go against him like this.

Because to be real, I don't wanna see KO lose.

Like, I don't necessarily want revenge the same way as the other guys.

Don't get me wrong, I definitely wanna beat him and I *know* KO wants to *destroy* us.

But that's all pride. That's competition stuff.

At the end of the day, I don't want any of the people in my life to lose anything else.

Not a game.

Not their spot on the team.

And definitely not their life.

More than I wanna win, I don't wanna lose.

Anyone.

Anymore.

There's barely room to lace up your sneakers. Man, there's hardly room to breathe, that's how packed this gym is. My bad, this *arena*. I was at the state finals both years D led our high school—he was only a freshman the first time, but you wouldn't know the way he played, and that place was at max capacity.

But this is my first time being in a building this big where I'm a part of the thing, too—and it feels mad different. How it smells. How it feels. How it sounds. All of it. Like, this is for real the first time I thought, *Dang, is it safe to have this many people smooshed in one place? Like, what if there's a fire? What if we gotta . . . evacuate or whatever.*

Ha. Not to be depressing. Just saying that's how wild it is in here.

Like when you watch the Final Four or NBA Finals wild.

People are hype like they've been building up that way for days, weeks, months.

"How many people you think in here right now?" Zay asks, reading my mind.

I shrug. "Bro, I don't even know. A few thousand?" I guess.

DJ shakes his head. "Gotta be more than that."

J-Wu looks up from the bench, his eyes big, his earbuds in. "Yooo, dude on the radio just said there's, like, seven thousand people here! I can't even believe it!"

And look, no one appreciates J-Wu's timing more than me. Dude's always got perfect timing, on and off the court. Except we're all staring at him, trying not to crack up because he's yelling at us like we're not standing less than two feet away.

"Guys! Guys!" J-Wu scrunches his face like he can't

believe we're not having the same reaction. "Did y'all hear me? Seven stacks, y'all!"

"Bro, we hear you. You ain't gotta scream," Zay says, laughing.

"Whaaat?!" J-Wu says, even louder.

Zay reaches over and pulls out one of J-Wu's buds. "Bro, you screaming right now."

J-Wu grins, cheeks a little red now. "My bad, fellas." And then the whole team's laughing.

Well, *almost* the whole team.

Meeks is relacing his kicks for the fiftieth time since we got here an hour ago. Meeks ain't even cracked a quarter smile all morning. Not at team breakfast, even though Ms. Carter surprised us with *real* bacon, crispy on the outside, chewy on the inside, the way we like it. Not after we all climbed onto the bus and not during our pregame walk-through.

"Yo, y'all know what time it is. This what we worked for. This what we been grinding for, naw'mean?" Meeks says, his face turned down in a face I'm not sure I've seen him rock before. He's always a serious dude, no doubt. But right now, he looks *tight*. And not good tight. Tight like when your leg cramps and you can barely walk. Tight like the muscle shirts Special K rocks under his jersey.

Thousands of people making all the noise. You can't hear yourself think. Which means I've gotta be extra sharp today, gotta make sure the team stays calm. An environment like this? D said these were the spots that let you know what kind of team you had. When the crowd was raucous. When everybody was hostile.

I spot KO and offer him a pound—he stares at my outstretched fist for a second, but then he taps it. "Good luck, KO," I tell him, and he nods, mumbles it back to me, then drifts back toward his sideline.

"Yo, why you fraternizing with the enemy?" Special K asks me.

"Special K with the vocabulary," Zay says, woofing.

"This ain't warfare, bro," I say. "Do I wanna kick his butt up and down the court? A hundred. But do I gotta be unsportsmanlike to do that? Nah."

Zay nods his agreement.

Special K shrugs. "Whatever, man. As long as we come out with this W, I don't care if y'all invite that dude for a sleepover this weekend."

"Point blank, period," J-Wu adds. "Let's get it."

Locked arm in arm in a circle, we lock eyes, and you can see it—we're focused.

We've got our game faces on.

But also, we're smiling. Because yeah, this game is important, it's serious, it matters.

But also, it's fun, because this is the game we love.

"One huddle, one hustle, one head, one heart!" we shout together in front of our bench.

We win the tip, and it's obvious our team's got a different energy. You can tell we know we belong here. That not only can we give the Wolves a good fight, we can beat them.

Even Meeks's weird pregame jitters seem to have disappeared—he's matched up against KO, and they're going at it, back and forth. KO scores on a ridiculous crossover at the top of the key, leaving Meeks in his dust for an easy scoop lay-in. And then Meeks fakes the crossover, gets KO to bite, before coolly knocking down a stepback jay.

Halfway through the second quarter, the game's tied at 34 all and DJ skies for a rebound over a defender twice his size, but when he lands, he comes down awkwardly and has to come outta the game. The tourney trainer tapes DJ's ankle on the sideline, and DJ tries to tough it out but it's obvious he's afraid to put weight on it.

"Meeks, you slide over to point. DJ, you're a gamer and you know I love it, but your teammates are gonna show up for you now."

DJ's frustrated, but he does his best to hide it. He nods to Meeks. "Light 'em up."

Meeks winks. "Don't worry. I got you."

Meeks gets another Wolves defender on a switch, KO wanting to check Meeks, but also afraid to leave sharpshooter Terry open.

"Go to work, Meeks," I shout from the bench. "The lane's open."

A thing Kiara and I noticed—Meeks shoots a high

percentage everywhere on the court, but he's converting at an unbelievable 70 percent of his attempts in the middle of the paint—a stat I've been reminding him of before, during, and after every game.

He fakes left, then right, jab, jab, rocks his defender to sleep, then spins back to the middle of the lane for a ten-foot jump shot.

We're up two now—and we're only getting started.

Soon everybody's chipping in. J-Wu knocks in back-to-back elbow jumpers. Special K shows off the running hook he's been perfecting in practice, hitting two of three attempts. And Terry's stroke has never looked better. He nails four treys.

The Wolves aren't sure what to do. They struggle with man-to-man, switch to a 2-3 zone, but we break that easily with great spacing and ball movement.

"Keep sharing the ball," Coach encourages, clapping in the huddle during a Wolves time-out. "You guys are playing great, but we've been in this position before and went flat. Keep up the energy."

Zay blows a Wolves defender up on a hard screen, springing Terry free for a corner three, *chu-kaa*. Next possession, we run the same exact play, except on the other side of the floor with Special K setting the pick, and again Terry splashes from distance.

The whole game I've tried not to pay too much attention to the scoreboard, but I can't help myself as our points start to pile up. On the other side, KO's doing his best to keep his team in the game, but our double-teams are frustrating him. When he keeps the ball, he puts up a terrible, contested shot. When he gives the ball up, his teammates jack up bricks, their confidence draining with every miss.

Ninety seconds before halftime, we've got the Wolves on their heels, with a commanding fourteen-point lead. You can see it in their players' eyes—they look broken.

And that's when it happens.

Meeks tries to run KO into a pick before Special K can set his feet, and Meeks steps on Special K's foot, twisting his ankle and falling to the ground.

Coach calls a time-out, and the tournament athletic trainer and physician race over to Meeks. Our whole team crowds around him, but Coach tells us to give him some space. "Yo, you all right, Meeks?" Special K keeps asking. He's rubbing his head, like maybe he wants to cry, his face in a tight knot. "Meeks, c'mon, man, you okay? My bad, bro. I'm sorry. I'm sorry."

Coach guides Special K away. "It's not your fault," I hear Coach say. "These things happen. He's gonna be okay."

And Coach is right. Meeks will be okay, but it's not gonna be in this game.

"Who's gonna run point?" Terry asks.

Coach nods. "You."

"Me?" Terry says. And I know what he's about to say—*I don't got the handles, Coach.* But I cut him off.

"You got this. Just play within yourself. Don't try to do

too much," I assure him.

But Terry's right—point guard isn't his game. He's an off-the-ball player. And the Wolves outscore us by five heading into halftime. Our double-digit lead is now down to nine.

"What are we gonna do, Coach? No offense, but Terry's not a point guard. He's a shooter," Zay says.

"We've come too far to let this lead slip away," J-Wu says.

Coach clasps his hands together. Turns toward me. And I expect him to ask me for a statistic, some weakness we can try to exploit. But instead he says, "Tone, you ready?"

"Ready for what?"

"I'm putting you in the game," Coach says. "If you're ready."

I shrug. "Coach, I'm not even on the roster. You can't just put me out there and—"

Kiara smiles. "You *are* on the roster, Tone. Every team gets to carry an injured reserve spot. Guess who's ours?"

Before I can answer, the whole team is surrounding me, patting me on the back, rubbing my shoulders, shouting encouragement at me from all directions.

"This is your time, Tone," Zay says. "You earned this."

"You've got the handles. You know how this team runs as much as anyone," Kiara says. "So go prove it on the court."

And I'm almost psyching myself up for it until I remember something kinda important.

"Umm, guys," I say. "I don't have a jersey."

Meeks pulls his off and pushes it into my chest. "Now you do."

I'm putting up a few warm-up shots when KO, shaking his head, slinks over. "Meeks can't go? DJ?"

"Nope," I confirm. "It's down to me."

KO shrugs. "You'll be all right. Play your game. Run the sets."

My face scrunches up. Is KO . . . helping me? "You feeling okay, man?"

KO shrugs again. "It doesn't matter if it's you or Meeks or whoever. We're still gonna win this game."

"There's the KO I know," I say, laughing.

And then it's game time.

I try to push the nerves down, but when I walk onto that court *as a player*, I can't help it—I've got mad butterflies in my stomach. The fact that Dad, Big Mama, Munka, and Tasha are screaming like the house is on fire isn't helping.

"That's my brooooootheeeeeeer!" Munka shouts.

"Tone, you got this," Big Mama yells, clapping.

"Play your whole butt off," Tasha chimes, laughing.

Terry stops beside me. "You good?"

I point to my stomach. "Bro, I'm feeling it."

He nods. "This ain't anything different than playing at Paradise. This is what D was always talking about. About staying ready for the moment. You're built for this, Tone. Read the defense and get us in the right sets. Take care of the ball."

"You make it sound so easy."

"Because we believe in you," Coach says, suddenly appearing on my other side.

The whistle blows and the third quarter begins, and I bring the ball up the court, the whole time I'm thinking, *Just don't mess up. Just don't mess up.*

I call a screen for Terry, but I meet his eyes and give a slight nod toward the baseline, and instead of sprinting out to the three-point line, Terry backdoors the screen, his defender caught shading Terry for the three-pointer is two steps too late, as Terry dashes toward the hoop for a nifty reverse layup.

"What I tell you?" Terry yells, dapping me up as we race back up the floor on defense. "Play your game."

I turn the ball over on the next play, trying to squeeze the ball into a tight window inside to Zay. "That's my bad," I say as the Wolves gobble up the pass and sprint ahead for a layup of their own.

"What I always tell you?" Zay asks me.

"Make it up?" I say back.

"You asking me, or you telling me?"

I nod. "I'll make it up."

"My dude," Zay says, punching me in the shoulder. "Let's go to work."

And we do, but the Wolves are back to playing like the Wolves we expected—super aggressive and super skilled. Back and forth both teams go, trading baskets, and at the end of the third, we're still up seven.

But then we go cold to start the fourth. No, not just cold. Ice cold. Glacier cold. Polar-bear-poop cold. We begin the quarter connecting on only one of our first eight attempts.

Meanwhile, the Wolves are red-hot.

Halfway through the fourth, Special K and I spring the perfect trap on KO—he has nowhere to go with the ball—but then he splits the two of us, spins around J-Wu and Terry, euro-steps past Zay, and shakes free for an acrobatic layup.

"Wow," I hear myself say.

"Dude's nasty," J-Wu admits.

"So cold," Zay chimes.

"Y'all gonna admire the man's work, or you gonna guard him?" Special K says. "Don't matter how fancy it is. It's still only worth two points."

"You right, you right," I say. "Let's get it."

But we still can't buy a hoop, and with three minutes left in the game, we're down seven. Only thing even keeping us that close is the fact that the Wolves are in foul trouble and we're knocking down free throws.

During a time-out, Coach doesn't hold back. "This is it. This is what we've been working our tails off for. Who cares if we miss the shot? We can't control how the ball bounces, but what we can control is effort and hustle and tenacity. Y'all wanna win, right?"

"Yes, sir!"

"I said, y'all wanna win, right?"

"Yes, sir!"

"Don't tell me," Coach says, drawing up a double screen. "Show me."

We respond with seven points unanswered, tying the score.

But then KO pokes the ball away from J-Wu and on a breakaway elevates for the most vicious dunk you'll ever see a fourteen-year-old kid punch. The crowd roars louder than the ocean. KO beats his chest, his head tossed back in a howl.

"Wolf pack. Wolf pack. Wolf pack," the Wolves fans chant all around the gym.

Coach calls our last time-out and smiles when we hustle over to the sideline. "We got them on the ropes. Do y'all feel that?"

"We're still down two, Coach," J-Wu says.

"What you see out there, Tone?" Coach asks me.

"Run a pick for Terry. If the shot isn't there, he swings it inside to Zay or Special K."

Coach nods. "You heard your point guard. Let's go. Hands in." The whole team thrusts their hands into the middle of the circle. "One huddle, one hustle, one head, one heart!"

"One huddle, one hustle, one head, one heart," we repeat.

"Break us down, Tone," Coach says.

"*Finish* on three," I yell. "One, two, three . . ."

"FINISH!"

We break huddle and are headed back onto the floor when Coach pulls me aside. "This is what you worked for. This is what you prepared for. This moment. Except now it's yours for the taking. So, go take it, Tone."

"I got you, Coach."

We run the play to perfection, Terry's got the wide-open three lined up, but KO gets a finger on the shot and it ricochets away. J-Wu dives on the floor to recover, but it squirts from his grip. Zay lunges at it, tips it backward, just before it sails out of bounds. Special K gets a hand on it, dribbles toward the lane, the entire Wolves team collapsing into the paint around him. Special K spins, but the Wolves are swarming, and he heaves a crosscourt pass to Terry.

Terry fakes a three and dives into the paint. I point to the shot clock.

To the game clock.

"Shoot the ball, Terry," I scream. "Shoot the ball!"

But the ball's already out of his hands.

Except it's not headed toward the hoop.

It's spiraling toward me.

Now Terry's screaming for me to shoot. I hear Coach and Kiara. Zay crashing the lane for a possible tip-in. I hear Dad and Munka, Tasha and Big Mama. Everybody screaming the same thing. "Shoot! Shoot!"

The ball hits me soft in my hands.

Glides into my palms.

My feet leave the floor, my defender leaping with me, his

hand outstretched for the block, I fade back, back, back . . .

Everything slowing down.

I glance at the sideline, and there in the stands I see him.

D.

He's smiling and I can't hear him but his lips are moving. He's saying, *That's game. That's game.*

I smile back and let the ball go.

It spins up, rotating toward the basket the way I've watched it a million times.

The whole arena falls hush.

The defender falls on top of me, and we collapse onto the court.

I can't see the ball.

But then I hear my favorite sound in the world—

*Chu-kaa.*

And then everything unfreezes and my teammates and my family and my friends are going wild, are lifting me up, carrying me around the court.

But me—my eyes are on the lone figure, standing by the exit doors.

He smiles.

"That's game," I say quietly as he disappears through the door. "That's game."

# 40

And you'd think the hard work was over. That it had paid off into one of the—if not *the*—biggest victories of our lives. That we'd reached the top of the mountain and now was a time to celebrate and be happy, to ease up and slow down.

That now we could take a breath and relax.

Ha, that's because you don't have Coach James in your life.

The whole team's on the bus to go home, and we're wild loud. We're geeked. We're laughing and cracking jokes and we're all, *Yo, did you see that block? That was vicious!* We're so pumped. We're like, *Yo, but that steal and reverse layup in the fourth quarter, that was nasss-ty, bro. That needs to be on a poster.*

We're tossing the game ball back and forth across the aisles, and we're singing and rapping along to the music blasting from Zay's stereo. And we're making plans for the last bit of summer we've got left.

And then Coach climbs on board, and we yell, "Coach Jay's in the house!" And we start cheering and pumping our arms. Some of us are barking. And now we're pounding the seats in front of us with our fists, stomping our feet, and we're chanting "MVP! MVP! MVP!"

Coach smiles and nods. Holds up his hand for us to be quiet, and someone snaps the music off, too.

Coach takes a few steps to where DJ's sitting and points right to DJ's chest, and he says, "MVP." And then Coach turns to the other side of the aisle where Zay's sitting and Coach points to Zay's chest and says, "MVP." And Coach does that to every single person on our bus, including Kiara, and then the driver, and Zay's mom.

And then Coach stands in the middle of the bus and holds out his finger and points at everyone again, like he's casting a spell on us. "We've had some ups and downs. We've lost games we should've won and won games we should've lost. We've practiced until we wanted to throw up. We've thrown up. We've fallen into beds exhausted, wiped out, knowing that the very next day we had to do it all over again. We've studied game film. We've studied our opponents. We've studied each other. We've had a next-man-up mentality. We prepared and played each game like it was our very last. We. *We.* Not me.

*We did that.* Which is why *we won*. Because we don't have *one* MVP. And I'm beyond proud of us. Of each of you. Thank you. For not giving up. For believing in me, yourselves, and each other. One huddle!"

"One huddle!" we echo.

"One hustle!"

"One hustle!"

"One head!"

"One head!"

"One heart!"

"One heart!"

"One huddle, one hustle, one head, one heart!"

"One huddle, one hustle, one head, one heart!"

"Ladies and gentlepersons, it is with great pleasure and the utmost pride that I present to you, your now-reigning AAU national champions!"

Everyone goes wild. Coach grinning as hard as any of us.

Coach raises his arms for us to be quiet, and again every sound leaves the bus, so silent it's like you can hear lungs inflating, hearts beating.

"But here's the thing about being champions," Coach continues. "It's easy to think that winning the chip is like reaching the very top of the mountain, yeah? You look down and you see just how high you climbed. You realize how much you overcame to make this summit. And you should be proud of yourselves. Because we know it wasn't easy. So yeah, we take a moment to enjoy the view way up here. We earned it. We deserve it . . ." Coach's voice trails off. His eyes scanning up and down every row, like he's searching for something or someone. "But also," Coach continues, "the thing people like you and I know about climbing mountains? Is that there's always a taller one waiting for you. Because real, professional mountain climbers? They savor the view where they're at, but also they're already planning their next ascent."

DJ nods, and Zay claps. "Preach, Coach."

"So I'm not sure about y'all, but me? I'm not satisfied with one great mountain climb. Anybody can climb one. But you wanna be different? You wanna prove that it wasn't a fluke? That you've got what it takes? You better start climbing that next mountain. Are y'all with me?"

"Yes, Coach!"

"Nah, I don't think y'all really want it. I said are y'all with me?"

*"Yes, Coach!"*

"Climb! Climb! Climb!" Coach James bellows out.

And we're with him, just like we promised. "Climb! Climb! Climb!"

Because, yes, we're gonna enjoy this moment—we earned it. But Coach is right. We're not anywhere near finished. This here? This is just the beginning. Yeah, we're not done conquering mountains. Nope. Not even close.

But the question is, are y'all with us?

# 41

After the championship, the news hits like a hammer.

Ramona Shelley strolls along the chain-link fence that surrounds Paradise Court, her hands clasped together, her eyes staring right at us, like she can see us through the TV screen.

It is exactly three months to the day since tragedy struck in Oasis Springs, rocking the entire Greater Milwaukee community, and indeed, the nation, when prep phenom, perpetual honor student, and the second-ranked high school basketball player in the country Dante Oscar Jones was gunned down not thirty yards away from his home, eventually dying on the very court where the star-in-the-making worked tirelessly, day and night, rain or shine, refining his craft, perfecting his game.

Tasha looks confused. "Wait, that's D! How come D's on the TV? What's happening?"

Big Mama shushes her. "I'll tell you in a sec, baby."

TONY: D was my best friend and one of the best people I know. He didn't deserve to die.

RAMONA: That's Tony Washington, best friend and fellow Oasis Springs resident, who was on his way to meet Dante to run basketball drills on this court—Paradise Court, as it's known by residents—when he heard the first shot ring out. Thirteen-year-old Tony ran as fast as he could, hearing four more shots as he raced down the halls of his Tower apartment, through the Oasis Springs square, and onto the court—where the young man he called his brother lay dying in a pool of his own blood . . .

TONY: I think that's why we're all so hurt and afraid. Because if an officer can just take away D's life like it's nothing, when D was easily one of the most gifted, most celebrated, and most selfless people in this whole city, in this whole state, well, what's gonna stop them from taking my life?

RAMONA: I . . . I wish I had a good answer, Tony.

TONY: The people who live here are tired of being judged just because we don't make as much money. Our lives still matter. Our lives are still valuable. We're not asking for any special treatment. All we're asking is to please stop gunning us down a few feet from where we lay our heads at night. I'm saying, when are y'all gonna start treating us like real people?

TERRY: What happened to him wasn't right. We all know that. He wasn't a threat. He didn't have any weapons. He was a good kid, and I should know . . .

RAMONA: Meet thirteen-year-old Terrance Jones, known to family and friends as Terry. If you're wondering if Terry's related to the victim, well . . .

TERRY: Yeah, Dante was my big brother. But this is more than just blood ties, you know? 'Te was the best role model you could ever have. He was a dude who always went about his business the right way, you know? He never skipped steps, never took shortcuts. All that he had, he earned.

RAMONA: What is it you especially want people to know about your older brother, Terry?

TERRY: I want people to know him for what he did with his life, not for being on the wrong side of a bullet. Dante taught me everything. How to take care of people. How to work hard in school. People don't know that about him. They just keep saying he was a baller, a great athlete. But my brother had a 4.0 GPA. He was in all honors classes and taking classes at the community college, too. He was a beast on the court, for sure. No one could stop him. But he was just as much as a force off the court, too. I miss you, D. I love you, D.

RAMONA: Many Oasis Springs residents uttered those same sentiments. We love you, Dante. Everyone loved Dante, they said. Including his coach, former NBA All-Star and Milwaukee hoops icon Hunter James.

COACH JAMES: Dante was more than a great basketball player. He was a legend. Imagine that, being a teenager but you're universally respected and beloved. Dante was a giant here, but his impact reached far beyond Wisconsin. You got people in Ethiopia and Sudan and China and Italy, watching his games on ESPN, following his season, checking his stats. Watching his highlights on YouTube. But you'd never know any of this, and he'd be the last person to tell you. He didn't even wanna do that cover shoot. Dante wasn't flashy. He didn't care about fame or clout.

RAMONA: But Coach, respectfully, some people will say, c'mon, this kid couldn't have been this good. There must be something we're missing. Another side, a darker side, to Dante that no one wants to talk about now that he's passed.

COACH JAMES: Did Dante make mistakes? Of course. He's a teenager. He's human. But I challenge you to find one person who'd honestly say a bad thing about that kid.

RAMONA: I've talked to a lot of people, I have, and it's been all good. Oh, wait, he got a detention once for being late to school or something, I think, earlier this year . . .

COACH JAMES: I gave him that detention. He was twenty seconds tardy to practice.

RAMONA: C'mon, Coach, twenty seconds?

COACH JAMES: Twenty seconds and I'd do it again the same way.

RAMONA: You're tough, Coach. No mercy, huh? Not even for a first offense?

COACH JAMES: Mercy? Mercy? These people out here aren't showing mercy to Black and brown boys, whether they got zero offenses or not. The tragic part is, it's not D's fault. It's not our kids' fault that we gotta rob them of their innocence. Our sons and daughters don't get to be kids and only have kid problems. No, they gotta be told how to act around police, how to behave even when they're not sure they're being watched, because even the slightest offense is enough for someone to justify taking their lives? You tell me: Where's the mercy in that?

RAMONA: If you could talk to the grand jury tasked with deciding whether to indict Officer Truman, what would you tell them?

TONY: I'd say there's nothing you can do to bring him back, but you can make sure Officer Truman doesn't kill another innocent person. That's what D would want. Justice.

RAMONA: You told me earlier that you feel as though Dante's still here with you?

TONY: With all of us, yeah.

RAMONA: Explain that.

TONY: Sometimes at night, when it feels like everybody in the world's asleep except me, and the pop of those gunshots starts replaying in my brain, I shut my eyes tight and I try to block out all the noise, until every other sound fades away. And that's when it happens . . .

RAMONA: What happens?

TONY: I hear him.

RAMONA: Dante?

TONY: Yeah. I hear his ball snapping in the net. I hear him sinking jump shots all over Paradise.

RAMONA: How does that sound?

TONY: Like, chu-kaa. Chu-kaa. Chu-kaa.

RAMONA: Wait, like chu-kough. No. I'm sorry. [laughing]

TONY: Chu-kaa.

RAMONA: Chu-krr. Chu-krr. Oh no, I give up. I can't do it.

TONY: It's okay. No one can do it like D.

And then OS disappears, and we're back to a live, solo shot of Ramona.

"And now we stand on the courthouse steps, eagerly awaiting the grand jury's decision, which I'm told should come down any sec— Hold on." Ramona holds her hand to her ear like someone's speaking into it and she needs to hear every word. She nods and looks at the camera straight on. "News has just come down. It's official. Officer Truman has been indicted."

And I imagine everyone in OS watching the news right now; I can almost hear them cheering and hollering and jumping up and down on those old wooden floors, happiness and hope ringing out from every Tower.

But inside this house, inside Big Mama's living room, we don't whoop or high-five or cheer. Because for us, it's not about winning something. We know that no matter what happens with Officer Truman, we still lost the most.

I don't know, maybe they decide he's not guilty and he gets to go back to his old life.

Or maybe they find him guilty and he goes to jail.

Either way, he's still here.

None of what happens now will bring D back.

Still, it's a start. And like Coach says, *You gotta start somewhere.*

Tasha sighs super dramatically, sounding like a big balloon deflating. "*Now* can you tell me what's happening?"

"Hopefully, justice," I answer.

Big Mama nods and repeats, "Hopefully, justice."

"For D?" Tasha asks.

"And for all of us," Big Mama says, still nodding, her hand finding mine and squeezing.

"Finally," Tasha says, like she's exhausted.

*Finally.*

# 42

It's late afternoon, and Big Mama's still at work when Dad hits us in our family group text:

**From Dad**

On my way. Double-check you got all your stuff.

Not long after, Dad's standing inside the front door and we're all grabbing our bags and suitcases and pillows and pushing out through the door and down the porch stairs.

The family van's parked in the driveway, and we head toward the back hatch to pile our stuff inside. Except there's a surprise waiting for us, hiding back there.

"Hi, babies," Mom says softly, like how she does when

she thinks we're sleeping and she's hovering above us, kissing our foreheads good night.

We explode into the biggest family group hug ever.

And we've got so many questions we wanna ask, but none of that matters.

Because *why* or *how* doesn't matter nearly as much as *when* and *what*.

Because *when* is happening right now.

Because *what* is love. The kind that doesn't need any explanations, or answers, or *I'm sorrys*. The kind of love that sticks to your ribs. The kind of love that shadows you so hard, wraps you up so good, you don't know where you start and where it ends.

The kind of love with no *ends*.

That shines just as bright on Other Days as it does Good Days.

The kind you depend on.

The kind that holds you all together even when you're apart.

I don't know when Dad found the time, but as soon as I step into the apartment, it hits me.

It hits us.

Not just that awesome feeling you get when you finally make it back home after being away for a long time—which is funny because before I couldn't wait to escape this tired place with its tired walls and tired clothes and tired ways, but after being away a while, now, being back here, it's like seeing an old friend for the first time in forever. You're all smiles and laughs and hugs and *I missed you so, so much.*

That's Munka, especially. Flying into her room, leaping onto her bed, kicking her legs like her blankets are the ocean and she's swimming, swimming.

Tasha clapping her hands, making up a song, using her own words set to a familiar beat—singing, *It feels good, yeah. It feels goooood, to be back home again.*

Mom standing in the doorway, still one foot in the hallway like she's not sure whether to go in or turn around, her face split down the middle between smiling and crying, she's wagging her head, covering her face with her hands held together like a tent, water slipping out between her fingers and sliding down to her chin, hanging there and dripping like thawing icicles onto our old wood floors.

Tasha stops singing to ask, "Mama, what's wrong? Why are you sad?"

Mom drags her hands down her face and smiles through the tears. "Mama's not sad. I'm the opposite of sad, baby."

"Then how come you're crying?"

"Because sometimes people also cry when they're so very happy." Mom's cheeks are two brown balloons floating up up up into the biggest smile.

And Tasha pretends to cry, too, now—and she's so convincing, Mom's like, "Baby, oh no, why are *you* crying?"

Tasha stops, her whole face beaming like a spotlight.

"Because I'm sooooo happy, Mama. I'm more happy than anything! And do you know how come?"

"I always wanna know whatever you wanna say, baby."

"No, Mama, you gotta say *how come*."

Mama laughs. "How come?"

"Because I love being here. Back home. But also it's like Dad said, *Home isn't a place, home is family*. And you're back home now. So now we've got our home again!"

More tears fall from Mom's face, but she doesn't move to wipe them. She lets them race down either cheek, and they meet in the middle of the underside of her chin, like the strings of a hat to tie together. And she stoops down, her arms wide, and Tasha runs into them. I remember when that was me, when I was small enough to scoop up. But also it *is* me now. Because Mom's arms are wide enough for all of us. Dad's, too.

Because just like with ball, if you share, everyone wins.

And then just like that—life's almost back to normal.

Dad's sliding across the kitchen floor, singing and chopping vegetables. Mom's singing and stirring the rice. Tasha's standing on the kitchen chair, dancing with her babies. Munka's half laughing at Dad, half eye-rolling her phone because some girl keeps liking KO's pics.

I make a face. "Yo, why you even care about KO's . . . Ooooh. Wait, you crushing on KO? For real?"

Munka tries to punch me in the arm. But I sidestep her and she only catches air—leaving her phone unattended. I grab it off the table, and I dive outta the kitchen. Then she's chasing me around until she corners me in the living room.

"Give it up *now*," she orders.

I shrug. "Nah, I don't feel like it."

"*Tony.*"

"*Munka.*"

This standoff could go on for hours. We've done it before, trust me. But I don't know—today I'm in a charitable mood, so I cough it up and she pushes me onto the couch. "I can't stand you sometimes," she says. But she's not really mad. This is just what we do. This is just who we are together.

"Tony," Dad says, suddenly appearing in the living room.

I'm guessing he's gonna yell at me about messing with my sister, but he just settles into his green chair, aims the remote, and says, "You tryna watch *Space Explorers*?"

# 43

There's a whole world of kids who've never stepped outside the place they're born.

Who spend their whole lives at the same school, buying the same food at the same grocery store, walking the same sidewalks. For a lot of kids, the four blocks around their house *is* the whole world.

It's not their fault.

It's hard to go after a thing you don't even know exists.

Because if you don't know there's more out there, how will you know to go after it?

See, here's what I finally realized.

This story? It isn't about what D's life should've been,

what it could've been. Or about a community mourning the loss of one of its brightest stars. Or about exacting justice in D's name.

This whole time, it felt like maybe this wasn't even my story at all.

That maybe I was just a supporting actor in the story of D's life.

And it's not like that's necessarily a bad thing—like, there are way worse people to support than Dante Oscar Jones, no doubt.

Except the funny thing is, that's not how D would've wanted it.

If D were here, and he knew that I'd been funneling every decision through the *what would Dante do* filter, he'd be pissed; on some *Yo, this is YOUR life, Tone. Only you can live it, so . . . live it.*

And as always, he'd be right. This is *my* life. This is *my* story.

And my story, man, it's only getting started.

Yeah, I got knocked off my game for a minute.

Life set a hard pick that dropped me flat on my butt.

But I got back up.

I hustled, I worked, I didn't take a single play off.

I sweat. I cried. I laughed. I cracked jokes. I smiled. I drove hard to the paint. I boxed out and battled for rebounds. You knocked me to the ground and I stood back up strong in my sneakers, every time.

You see, my story's got plenty of hard parts; sharp parts that sometimes make me wanna scream: *I matter, too! I won't let you win! I won't let you beat me! Is this all you got?!*

It's got sad parts, the kind where you bury your face into your pillow to hide your wet eyes.

It's got happy parts, the kind where you can't stop smiling at the coach's daughter, where you see the insides of museums, where you find art that looks like you, that celebrates you, where you discover that the world isn't just the four blocks surrounding your house. There are entire worlds out there waiting for you. There are whole galaxies with moon pies and the best milkshakes you'll ever have in your whole *it's complicated* life.

Because life is a fast break coming right at you, but don't be scared, because you and me know how to get back in transition. How to stop the ball and force a turnover. We know how to turn good defense into great offense. How to swing the momentum in our favor. And now we've got the ball and we're sprinting toward our goal. And I promise you I'll always play the right way, so if you're open, I'm gonna hit you with the perfect pass, so be ready, yeah? But if the defender cheats your direction, then I know the ball's gotta stay with me.

The ball soft in my palms as my feet leave the court, leave the gym, until it's just me and the rim. Me busting through gravity. Flying. Soaring. Skying.

Me finishing strong, the ball floating off my fingertips up up up—

Spinning toward the metal rim, the nylon net.

Because all of us, everything on this earth, has a place where we belong.

A home that's waiting for you.

Because this ball is no different.

It lives in this hoop.

And before the game clock expires and the buzzer sounds, before your teammates tackle you, burying you in a mountain of celebration, before you cut down the net and blow a kiss to your family cheering in the stands, before you dump the cooler of energy drink all over Coach, before you tell Kiara thank you, before you tell D, *this is for you AND me*, before you come back down to earth, before you let your shooting hand fall to your side as the scoreboard flickers and clicks.

Before the final score is tallied.

When everything hangs in the balance.

When it's all on the line and it feels like anything's possible.

You smile.

You remember how you got here.

You remember the Ls you took.

And you know within every ounce of your soul that *yes, there are things we can never get back*. But also, there are things we can never lose.

And before you slip back into your bed, in the apartment that you share with the family that you love and trust and can't stand all at the same time.

When you lace your fingers behind your head and sink into your pillow.

When you box out all the noise until you hear your favorite sounds:

The ball *thwacking* against blacktop.

The gravel crunching beneath sneakers.

The swish of the sweetest stroke Paradise Court has ever seen—*chu-kaa, chu-kaa.*

You say, *That's game.*

You call, *Game.*

# ACKNOWLEDGMENTS

I would like to thank my children: Camary, JC, Mia, Ava, and Gia.

My wife, Andrea, who supported my vision of pursuing this process of bringing this book together. My community of Racine & the Butler Elite program. I was inspired by the realities that exist.

Last, my mentor Kobe Bryant. I promised him my second act would be better than my first, and I would use my platform for change.

—Caron Butler

I want to thank everyone who encouraged me to shoot my shot and chase my writing dreams. I want to thank my family and friends for believing in me, even when the game's on the line and time's expiring. Thank you to K & B for pushing me to be better, all the time. To my sister and nephew, to my parents, thank you for your love, no matter the game's final score. Seriously, I'd put my squad up against any team, any day, all day.

Thank you to Caron; I couldn't imagine a better teammate. Thank you to Ben Rosenthal, the best editor/coach in the game. Thank you to Beth Phelan for helping me get the playing time we've worked so hard for. To everyone at Katherine Tegen Books and HarperCollins Children's, thanks for helping us play *our* game.

But most importantly, to every kid: the ball doesn't have to be in your hands to impact the outcome, to make a big play. There are lots of ways to change the game. But you can do it. You *are* doing it. Keep grinding.

—justin a. reynolds